ONLY YOU

Kay Doherty

Case Holden hates his life. Made rich at a young age, he slipped into a lifestyle of partying with multiple boyfriends who only wanted to be with him for what he could give them. After confiding to his aunt that he's miserable, she extends an invitation for a visit. Case plans to spend the time in small town Clover City to reprioritize and plant his feet on the road to happiness. He does not expect the Clover City sheriff to step into his world and wreak havoc on his emotions.

Two years ago, after the death of his partner, Rawley Kane moved to Clover City, trading the painful memories and big city madness for a less stressful existence. Even as sheriff, his life is uncomplicated and quiet. That is until Case Holden rolls into town and reminds Rawley just how lonely he is, and of everything he's been missing.

Case is everything Rawley shouldn't want. The man has six boyfriends and a life back in Denver, not to mention he's quite a bit younger than Rawley. No matter what he tells himself, he can't get enough of the young man. And Case has made it clear Rawley is the only one he wants. Now if they could just get past Rawley's guilt and Case's insistent boyfriends, they just might stand a chance.

A NineStar Press Publication

Published by NineStar Press
P.O. Box 91792,
Albuquerque, New Mexico, 87199 USA.
www.ninestarpress.com

Only You

To all those who put their lives and mental health on
the line daily to keep us safe—thank you.

Acknowledgements

Like the main character of this novel, my brother and I suffer PTSD. We have it for very different reasons, but the effects it has on our lives are similar. I drew from our individual experiences and combined them to create Rawley's condition. Each person diagnosed with PTSD will suffer differently, with different symptoms and varying degrees of severity. After years of intense, psychologically painful therapy, my PTSD has become mild. My brother has a therapy dog to help mitigate the severity of his symptoms. It is a real illness with real treatment available if one recognizes the symptoms. If you think you suffer PTSD, seek out a professional for help. PTSD is *not* something to be ashamed of or embarrassed about.

Chapter One

SMOKE BILLOWED FROM beneath the hood of Case Holden's Mustang as he slowed, easing to the side of the road, where the engine gave a final rattle before dying. Case did his best to maneuver the car completely off the pavement to avoid getting hit by other vehicles. Rain was coming down in sheets, and he cursed when he felt one of his tires come to a sudden halt in the mud along the shoulder of the road. He was on a remote country byway and hadn't passed another car in quite a while, but he still didn't want to risk anyone knocking into his baby with the limited visibility caused by the downpour. This Mustang was his pride and joy. He had spared no expense when he bought the car, adding every luxury available. Though he was careful to keep it in pristine working order, this trip had pushed the vehicle to its limit.

Case didn't know a damn thing about cars. He had entrusted the Mustang's mechanical issues to one of his many boyfriends—a boyfriend who was just one of many reasons he was making this drive. Case had become a partying drunken slut in the past several years, hemorrhaging money. Now, because of choices made and paths taken, he was stranded in the middle of nowhere in the pouring rain. He lifted his cell phone out of the middle console and let out another string of expletives. There was no service and the battery was about two seconds from dying.

When he finally managed to arrive at his aunt's house, he was going to have a discussion with her about her choice of address. The last time he visited his Aunt Sylvia, he had fallen in love with her cozy house and the massive amount of land he'd been allowed to explore for hours on end. He didn't remember the drive being so long and desolate, though. Sylvia and her late husband, Ed, had bought the acreage with the hopes of starting a ranch, but that idea had died a quick death shortly after they had moved into the two-bedroom cabin. The house was situated at the edge of a forested area, with an awesome lake for fishing within walking distance, but the cabin itself had been in need of serious attention.

Two years and hundreds of thousands of dollars later, Sylvia and Ed had basically rebuilt the place. When Case last visited at age fifteen, it had been state of the art with all the modern amenities and taken every dollar his aunt and uncle had put away for the ranch. It had been ten years since Case was out this way. He'd slept in the back seat for the majority of the drive during that family trip, which he now knew he preferred after being alert, painfully aware of every boring mile traveled. It was mind-numbing. Case allowed the engine to cool for several long minutes before he turned the key in the ignition. The engine made an awful grinding noise but never caught. He gave a few more futile attempts before slamming his palms against the wheel in frustration.

"Damn, damn, damn. What the hell am I supposed to do now?" he yelled to the empty seats. He was out in bumfuck nowhere, alone, with a dead phone and a dead car. He was a city boy surrounded by the most up-to-date electronics, none of which were any use to him. He twisted in his seat and looked down the road behind him and then slowly turned to look out all the windows to assess his options and found zero. There were no houses, no traffic—nothing but rain and flat terrain as far as the eye could see. Admittedly, that wasn't all that far at the moment. He stuffed his phone into his bag, jerking his jacket on with angry motions. The chances of another car coming upon him and actually stopping were slim to none. Walking seemed to be his only option since he couldn't call anyone for help.

Case grabbed the strap of his bag and dragged it across the seat as he got out of the car. Once he was free from its confines, he slung the strap over his shoulder and locked the doors. Rain instantly soaked through his jacket, droplets sliding down his neck onto his chest and back, making him shiver. He stuffed his hands into his pockets, ducked his head against the occasional gust of wind, and started walking, hoping like hell there was a house or gas station or something with a phone in the near distance. After almost losing a shoe to the sucking mud that lined each side of the two-lane highway, Case decided to risk walking on the pavement. Since there hadn't been a car in recent memory, he figured he was safe.

Chapter Two

SHERIFF RAWLEY KANE massaged the stiff muscles of his neck with one hand as he maneuvered the steering wheel with the other. Despite the heavy rain, the truck's speedometer showed he was pushing fifty miles an hour. He'd driven on this highway almost daily for the past two years and was familiar enough with it to know the chances of another vehicle being on the road on a sunny day were small, let alone in a downpour. The population of Clover City just didn't go out in weather like this, and if they did, they knew the road just as well, if not better than he did. Worst thing Rawley had to worry about was a stray dog or a deer running out in front of him.

Bright gold winked in the distance so Rawley slowed the truck. As he drew closer, he realized the bright gold was a car on the side of the road. Rawley carefully eased alongside the vehicle, a Ford Mustang that was all kinds of fancy and all kinds of expensive. It was also empty. As he passed the vehicle at a crawl, he looked at the car through the side mirror and noticed the front passenger wheel was sucked pretty deeply into the mud. Rawley sighed as he stopped the truck right in the middle of the lane.

He wasn't about to pull off the pavement because the weight of his truck would sink him into the same mud the Mustang was mired in. A nice car like this no doubt belonged to some hotshot city dweller unfamiliar with country roads or driving too fast for the conditions. He flipped on the bar of police lights on top of his truck to alert any potential motorists he was stopped in the middle of the road. He mentally ran through the list of deputies who might be in the office as he picked up the radio.

"Ted, you in?" Rawley asked through the CB. He jotted down the Mustang's license plate number while he waited for a response.

"Yep. What's up, Kane?" was Ted's static reply.

Two years after being elected sheriff of Clover City, Rawley was accustomed to small-town informality. He had come from the Denver Police Department, broken and jaded, and hadn't adjusted all that quickly to the change. Now, the friendship and camaraderie of Clover was familiar, comfortable—he wouldn't trade it for anything. He eased his foot off the brake, allowing the truck to coast down the highway at a snail's pace while he scanned the surrounding area for the car's missing occupants.

"Can you let Dusty know we have a car stuck in the mud just south of McKesson's farm heading toward town?"

"He won't go out in the storm. Afraid of getting struck by lightning or some dumb shit. You know that," Ted said.

Rawley rolled his eyes. "Just tell him it's there. He can go get it later when it clears."

"All right, I'll call him. You on your way back?" Ted asked.

"I'm heading that way, but the car was empty, which means I've got a driver and possibly passengers missing in action. I may be awhile if they aren't on the road ahead."

"Roger that, boss man," Ted said.

Rawley set the radio back into the cradle as he pressed on the gas to increase his speed. His gaze slid across the rain-soaked terrain as he moved down the road, hoping to find the owner of the Mustang hunkered down under a tree or lumbering through the mud because he did not want a missing person investigation to deal with. Three miles down the road, he slowed once again when he caught sight of a man, hunched over against the rain, walking down the middle of the lane. The red and blues were still flashing, but he hit the button for the siren long enough to alert the person to his presence. The man turned to face Rawley as he skipped to the edge of the pavement, out of the way. Rawley unlocked the doors as he pulled up alongside the man. Without any encouragement, the guy opened the passenger door and climbed into the warm, dry cab of the truck.

"I've never been so happy to see a cop in my life," the man said.

He turned a radiant smile on Rawley, causing Rawley to momentarily forget how to breathe at the man's stunning beauty. He was young, handsome with dark hair made black by the rain, gray-blue eyes with thick, dark lashes, and he was thoroughly soaked. It had been years since Rawley had seen a man as beautiful as this one, and urges he thought he'd left behind in Denver once again stirred. Rawley shifted slightly in the seat as he cleared his throat.

"That your car back there?" Rawley asked with a backward jerk of his head.

"Yeah. Engine died. There was a grinding noise and smoke coming out of it," the man answered with a flourish of his hands Rawley assumed was to indicate smoke rising.

The man lifted the strap of his duffel bag over his head to push the bag to the floorboard between his feet. Rawley caught himself staring at the man's muscled bicep and thigh as the guy leaned forward. Rawley yanked his attention back to the windshield when the man straightened. He shut off the emergency lights and stepped on the gas.

"What's your name and where you headed?" Rawley asked as he pushed the truck up to speed.

"Case, and I'm going to my aunt's. She lives out here...somewhere," Case said, twirling his finger in a circle. "Hey, do you have a phone I can use to call her? What are the chances of me getting my car towed?"

"I've already called for a tow. Your car will end up in Clover when the storm blows over. As for a phone—here."

Rawley pulled his cell phone from his coat pocket, unlocked the screen, and handed it over to Case. He tried not to shudder from the hot tingles Case's touch ignited when their fingers brushed.

"Thanks," Case said as he worked the phone.

"Sure. I'm surprised you don't have one."

"I do, but the battery died." Case lifted the phone to his ear and waited.

"Having a streak of bad luck today," Rawley pointed out.

Case scoffed at the remark, and then muttered, "You don't know the half of it."

Chapter Three

THE PHONE RANG in Case's ear as he tried to covertly check out his rescuer. He'd had his fair share of run-ins with the law—most of them unpleasant experiences with homophobic cops—but so far, this guy seemed to be a genuinely nice man. Plus, he was handsome. He was much older than Case, with a day's worth of stubble over his cheeks and strong jaw, deep-brown eyes, and light-brown hair cut short, the thick strands standing up in sexy disarray. That was just what Case had noticed as he climbed into the truck. From the corner of his eye, he could see where jeans stretched tight over a muscular thigh. He couldn't stop himself from imagining what else the cop hid beneath his clothes. Case was usually attracted to pretty boys closer to his age, but this rugged-looking, older man was hitting all his hot buttons. A high feminine voice speaking into his ear yanked him back to the task at hand.

"Rawley, dear, it's been a long time," she said in greeting.

"Rawley? No, Aunt Sylvia, it's me, Case," he said.

Case rolled the cop's name over his tongue as he risked a glance at the man to give him another quick once-over. Rawley was an unusual name, but somehow, it seemed fitting.

"Casey? Why are you calling from the sheriff's phone? Is everything all right?" she asked.

Well, shit. Case rubbed his forehead. *I'm lusting after the damn sheriff. Could this day possibly get worse?*

"Everything's fine, Aunt Syl. My car broke down, and he just happened to find me. He told me the car is going to be towed to Clover later, but I need you to tell him how to get to your house," Case said.

"Oh, sweetheart, believe me, Rawley knows how to get to my house."

The way his aunt was talking, Case had to wonder just how well she was acquainted with the sheriff. Uncle Ed had been dead for five years, but Aunt Sylvia was still fairly young and lively. If Case found out he was salivating over his aunt's newest, much younger love interest, he was going to dig his eyes out of his skull. Case sighed quietly as he turned to look at Rawley.

"Aunt Sylvia says you know how to get to her house."

Rawley glanced at him before returning his attention to the wet road. "If your aunt is Sylvia Dawson, then yes, I do."

Case nodded as he turned to look out the passenger window. Propping his elbow on the narrow sill, he rested his chin in his palm. "Yeah, he knows where he's going. I'll see you in a bit."

"That's great, honey. Bye."

"Bye," Case mumbled to the dial tone and lowered the phone to his lap. Rather than allow his thoughts to wander into territory best not visited, Case decided to try conversation. "So, is Rawley your first or last name?"

"First," Rawley answered. Case raised his eyebrows and waited for Rawley to expound on that, like maybe including his last name, but there was only silence.

"You're the sheriff of Clover City?"

"Yes."

Again, he waited to see if the sheriff was going to add anything else, but Rawley remained silent. Case shook his head in irritation as he looked out the window at the passing scenery, mostly obscured by rain. This entire day, this entire trip, had been shit and it wasn't getting any better.

"Not one for conversation, are you?" Case mumbled to the window.

Case turned away from the dreary landscape outside the window to find Rawley watching him. They held each other's gazes for a moment before Rawley exhaled and refocused his attention to the road. Case swallowed hard as he directed his gaze out the front windshield. He could stare into those deep-brown eyes all day. Case wondered if Rawley's eyes were more expressive when he became emotional, if they darkened when he was aroused, but the thought was interrupted when Rawley decided to talk. His deep voice jolted him back to the present, and Case realized he was staring so he quickly averted his attention to the passing scenery.

"My name's Rawley Kane, Clover City transplant. Became sheriff two years ago, and in about two hours, you'll know more about me than I want you to. Sacrifice of a small town. Everyone knows your business.

You, on the other hand, are a stranger in my town, so why don't we talk about you?"

"Why two hours?" Case asked.

Rather than answer the question, Rawley picked up the radio. "Hey, Ted."

"All good?" A voice, presumably Ted, crackled over the radio.

"Yes. Found the driver and he's Sylvia's nephew. We'll be at her place in a few minutes. Have Dusty contact him there once he picks up the car, okay?" Rawley said.

"Sure thing, boss man." Ted disconnected, and Rawley set the handset back in the cradle.

Case broke the silence when he couldn't stand it any longer. He was a social creature by nature and he hated sitting quietly in a room full of people, especially when he was energized or anxious.

"Case Holden, currently unemployed, visiting my father's sister out here in the middle of nowhere in an attempt to get my head on straight. And right now, after everything that's happened today, I'm seriously questioning my sanity."

"Get your head on straight?" Rawley asked. "What does that mean, exactly?"

Case didn't want to admit to this gorgeous man, a cop no less, how he had allowed men, alcohol, and sex to take over his life or that he basically ran away because he had no idea how to break the cycle. He had made a lot of bad decisions that now felt like addictions, and during a phone call to his aunt, he had broken down, telling her how miserable he was. That's when she had suggested he come visit her in the country so he could have the time and space to figure out his life. Case had jumped at the chance to quit his lifestyle cold turkey.

"I needed to get away, make some changes in my life. I'm here to figure out how to do that," Case said.

Rawley made a sudden turn off the main highway onto a muddy, rutted road that had Case grabbing the dash for balance, heart beating wildly as he was jerked around on the seat. He was driving faster than Case thought was necessary, considering the conditions, and it was painfully jarring.

"Can you slow down?" Case asked after a particularly painful bump that had threatened to jam his head into the ceiling.

"Not unless I want to get stuck in the mud," Rawley answered and gunned the truck up a slight incline.

The truck launched over the top of the small hill and landed with a jolt that had Case shooting daggers at the sheriff, who was grinning slightly. The damn man was enjoying Case's discomfort. Once they entered the cover of trees a short distance down the drive, Case recognized his aunt's property and realized that if he'd been driving, he would have missed the turn off the highway.

Branches blocked some of the rain, and the closer they got to the house, the less rutted and muddy the road became. Shallow puddles were scattered around, but the worry about getting stuck in the mud was removed so Rawley slowed their speed. Case forced his fingers to relax around the door handle but refused to completely let go in case Rawley decided to gun it again. He was still casting annoyed glances at the man when the truck rumbled to a stop in front of the cabin. Aunt Sylvia was standing on the covered porch, waving as Case relinquished his hold on the door, snapped up his bag, and exited the truck.

"Casey Eugene Holden. Look at you all grown up and handsome," Aunt Sylvia said.

Case cringed at the use of his full name as he ran across slick mud and jumped over puddles to join his aunt on the porch. Aunt Sylvia immediately engulfed him in a crushing hug, despite the fact he was soaked head to toe. Case was always amazed at how strong the diminutive woman was; she was squeezing the life out of him. When she released him and saw that Rawley had followed him, she latched her viselike grip onto Rawley. Case took advantage of Rawley's momentary distraction to get a good look at the man. What he saw was six feet plus of rain-soaked, muscular deliciousness he would beg for a taste of if Rawley showed so much as an inkling of interest. Case groaned as he scrubbed his hands over his face and then threaded his fingers through his wet hair. He needed to keep thoughts like that from playing in his brain immediately because Sheriff Rawley Kane was off-limits, just like every other man in Clover City.

"Come on inside, both of you. I put some coffee on and pulled some towels out." Aunt Sylvia practically shoved the two of them through the front door. "Casey, drop your bag in the guest room and change into something dry. Some of your uncle's clothes are in the closet if you need anything."

She made shooing motions at him while pushing him toward the hall before going into the kitchen. When Case looked back over his shoulder, he noticed Rawley was still standing near the door, staring at him so Case ducked into the guest bedroom and closed the door. He spun to lean against it, dropping his bag to the floor with a dull thud. He was almost certain Rawley had been checking him out, but Case purposefully snuffed out the blossoming hope that idea created, because getting involved with someone new wasn't on the agenda, and he needed to remember that. Case bent down, picked up his bag, and tossed it on the bed, where he yanked it open, turning his focus away from piercing brown eyes filled with desire and toward getting into dry clothes.

Chapter Four

RAWLEY GROANED AS he tilted his head back to look at the popcorn ceiling and placed his hands on his hips. Case had just caught him staring at his ass. Maybe he'd get lucky and Case would assume he was straight like everyone else did, thinking Rawley was just watching him leave the room. Rawley hadn't had this problem in the two years since moving to Clover. Not a single man in town had come close to stirring his libido the way Casey Holden did, and he found he no longer knew how to handle it.

Rawley had considered coming out to the locals a dozen times, whenever some well-meaning mother attempted to set him up with their sweet but lonely daughter. He'd probably still be accepted, given there was already a gay couple living in town, but Rawley just didn't see the point. There was no one here he wanted a relationship with, and it wouldn't make a difference if he told Case he was gay. Case was a city boy. Once his little visit was over, he'd be going back.

Getting involved with Case would only leave Rawley feeling more alone than he already did, and the real kicker was that he got the impression Case would be on board with a short-term fling. Rawley had kept his reaction to the young man locked down, but he was acutely aware every time Case had glanced his way during the drive, which had been often. Even now, he could feel the heat of those gray-blue eyes sliding over his body. Sylvia returned to the room, carrying a mug of coffee and a bath towel draped over her arm, and handed everything to him with a smile.

"Dry off a little and have a seat," she said and then disappeared into the kitchen again.

Rawley set the mug on the coffee table and tossed the towel on the arm of the chair so he could remove his coat. He wasn't anywhere near as soaked as Case, but his hair was wet, his jeans damp in spots over the back of his thighs, butt, and ankles. He opened the front door to drape his coat over the stack of lawn chairs on the covered porch. Rain was still coming down in sheets, and he figured by the time he managed to extricate himself from Sylvia's hospitality, the dirt road back to the highway would be nothing but one long muddy puddle. Rawley closed the door with a sigh. His entire afternoon off had been hijacked by one hot, young, blue-eyed boy. Rawley returned to the chair and spread the towel over the seat as Sylvia joined him, carrying two additional mugs.

Rawley sat down, his wet jeans irritating his skin, and sipped his coffee. Sylvia sat on the sofa cushion the farthest away from him with a smile that made him a bit nervous. It was the smile of a scheming woman, and that always went badly for him. Case chose that moment to join them. His feet were bare, and he had changed into white-washed jeans that might as well have been painted on, paired with a plain white T-shirt that molded to his toned frame. His hair was still damp but cutely mussed like he'd just run his fingers through it. The overall effect was sexy as hell. Case took a seat in the only spot left for him, the end of the sofa nearest Rawley. Case rubbed his hands down his thighs and glanced at Sylvia quickly before speaking to Rawley.

"I pulled some of Uncle Ed's clothes out for you if you want to change into something dry. He was about your size, I think," Case said. He held Rawley's gaze for a moment before staring down at the coffee mug Sylvia pushed across the table in front of him. Warmth spread through Rawley's body at Case's thoughtfulness. He let his gaze slide down Case's body before staring into his coffee.

"Go ahead, Rawley," Sylvia urged. "We aren't going anywhere, and from the looks of the storm, you won't be leaving for a while, either."

Sylvia smiled at him over the rim of her mug, making his stomach roll with anxiety. He had the sense that the moment he was out of the room he would become the topic of conversation. Rawley pushed to his feet with a nod, intent on making this the quickest change of clothes ever. He yanked the towel off the chair and rushed down the hall to the guest bedroom. Case's bag sat on the foot of the bed; all the clothes inside had gotten wet, probably from Case's hike in the rain. Case had laid them out on the bed and over the chair to dry. The room already smelled like the man, making Rawley's dick plump against his zipper.

The damp jeans stuck to Rawley's skin as he peeled them off, followed by his underwear. Thanks to the direction of the wind, his backside had taken the majority of impact. The loaner pants were a bit too big in the waist so he removed his belt from his own jeans to hold them up, causing the fabric to bunch in places and dig into his abdomen. He wasn't comfortable, but he was dry.

Rawley tucked his phone and wallet into the pockets of his borrowed pants, and folded his wet jeans. After taking one last good inhalation of Case's subtle scent, he returned to the living room where Sylvia was laughing. She wiped a tear from her eye with one hand while holding her stomach with the other. Case watched his aunt with furrowed brow, shaking his head and appearing a bit offended. Rawley looked back and forth between the two as he went to the front door and opened it. He set his wet clothes on the porch beside the chair holding his coat, noting the rain had yet to let up, and then returned to his seat beside Case. Rawley curbed his curiosity in favor of another healthy swallow of still-hot coffee.

"It wasn't that funny, Aunt Sylvia. It was actually very embarrassing," Case said, folding his arms over his chest, though his brow had smoothed out a degree.

Sylvia's phone rang from the kitchen and she rose to answer it. "I'm sure it was, honey. I'm not laughing at you, just the situation. Think about it. You'll laugh, too," she said over her shoulder. She picked up the phone from the kitchen counter and then disappeared into the adjoining room Uncle Ed had set up as a study. Case rubbed his hands down his thighs as he broke into a huge smile.

"Yeah, I guess it was kind of funny," he muttered to himself and laughed. Rawley sent a silent thank-you to the cosmos that Ed's pants were too big. The loose fit gave his dick room to swell without being noticed because, damn, Case Holden's smile was a thing of beauty, his laughter light and genuine.

"Will you tell me what was so embarrassing and funny?" Rawley asked softly as he sipped his coffee.

"God, no," Case answered with a shudder, though his smile never faded. "Thanks for the rescue today. I'll never let my phone die again. I need technology to survive."

"It's my job—protect and serve and all that—but you're welcome," Rawley said. He would have helped Case even if he hadn't been sheriff, but he needed to establish some distance. Making this whole situation all about doing his job allowed him that.

Rawley tore his gaze away from Case when he realized he was watching every little movement and expression Case made. Checking the weather suddenly became important, so Rawley jumped to his feet, walked to the large picture window overlooking the porch, and pulled his cell phone out to activate the weather app. The sooner he could get away from this guy, the better. Outside, the rain was still coming down, though it did seem to be easing a bit. His truck was surrounded by shallow puddles. Getting the truck turned around and back down the rutted, uneven driveway wouldn't be impossible, but he'd just gotten into dry pants so running out to get soaked again didn't appeal to him.

Chapter Five

CASE LEANED BACK into the sofa cushion and stretched his feet out under the coffee table. He couldn't relax while Rawley was in the house, but he could enjoy the view he had of Rawley's backside. The pants were too loose for him to see the definition of Rawley's thigh or butt muscles, but that was probably a good thing. Case didn't need to be teased with what he couldn't have. Case had suffered his fair share of crushes on straight men over the years. He would generally allow himself to fantasize about the man for a week or two before forcing himself to move on, and he would do the same with Sheriff Kane.

"Don't think the Mustang would've gotten you down this driveway today." Rawley's deep voice resonated inside Case. He thought about the ruts and mud they'd driven over and knew Rawley was right. Even without the rain, he wasn't sure his car would do well. The 'Stang was built for speed and pavement, not rutted dirt roads in the country.

"Yeah. Should be interesting trying to get in and out of here, but I don't have a lot of driving planned. When do you expect it will be fixed?" Case asked, jumping at the chance to have a conversation that steered him away from his attraction to the cop.

Rawley shrugged in response as he returned to his seat, shoving his phone into a back pocket. "Dusty will tow it later today when the rain stops and probably take a look at it tomorrow. He doesn't usually work on Sundays unless it's an emergency. Guess timing depends on what's wrong with it, the parts it needs, and your ability to pay for the repairs."

"I can pay. Is this Dusty top-of-the-line? That car's never been to a second-rate mechanic. I take care of my girl," Case said. If Dusty turned out to be some low-tech, used-parts kind of mechanic, Case would look for someplace else to get the Mustang fixed.

"Sure, you take care of her," Rawley scoffed. "That's why she's currently broken down and stuck in the mud on the side of the highway."

Case crossed his arms as he clenched his jaw. He'd needed to get away from Derek, his mechanic and on-off boyfriend, but he didn't want Derek's work being insulted. Case glanced over his shoulder toward the study, wondering how much longer Aunt Sylvia was going to take, because maintaining a conversation with the sheriff was becoming difficult. He gazed out the picture window and became annoyed with the rain. If it weren't for the weather, the trying man in front of him would be long gone by now.

"Don't worry, city boy. We have plenty of bailing wire and gum," Rawley drawled in an exaggerated hillbilly twang and then shook his head. "I'm sure Dusty can scrape up a fix for you."

Rawley held Case's stare without blinking. Rawley's expression was serious, but he had to be joking. Case tried to place where he was on a mental map in an attempt to find a nearby town to have his car towed. When Aunt Sylvia returned to the room and reclaimed her seat, clapping her hands and smiling, both men turned to her.

"What?" Case asked. The last time he'd seen Aunt Sylvia this excited had been at his house in Denver two years ago, planning a surprise party for his father's fortieth birthday.

"Jake and Ryan are lifesavers," she said. "They said the annual barbecue can be held in their barn." The declaration was lost on Case because he didn't know who those men were, but he smiled and nodded anyway.

"Great! That barn is massive. Once the tractors are moved out, we could fit the band, tables, chairs, and the food prep equipment inside," Rawley said.

"Exactly, and I think there might even be room for a makeshift dance floor," Aunt Sylvia said excitedly. She turned her attention to Case. "I help with the yearly gathering. It was set to happen next Saturday, but the field caught fire last week. We've been going crazy trying to find another venue."

"Oh. Congratulations," Case said. "Who is *we*?"

"The Clover City Social Committee," Aunt Sylvia answered.

It didn't surprise him that his aunt would be part of something like that. Even as a child, he remembered her being very outgoing and friendly. No matter where she went, people flocked to her. His father called Aunt Sylvia a radiant spirit that would never dim. Watching her now, Case could see it. He'd never really looked before.

Case eased back on the sofa, sipping his lukewarm coffee, as the rain fell outside the large window across from him while Aunt Sylvia and Rawley discussed the upcoming gathering and all the people attending. Case's muscles relaxed and his mind wandered to the childhood days he'd spent here with his parents. His life had been simpler then, when his grandfather was still alive and Case had nothing more to worry about than what he would wear on his first day of school. A sharp slap across his upper arm jolted him back to the present.

"Ow."

"I'm talking to you," she said.

"Sorry," he said, rubbing the sting from his skin as he scowled at his aunt.

"Well, as I was saying, I forgot to tell you earlier that I called Dusty after I hung up with Jake. He said he'll tow your car later this afternoon, and you can stop by the shop tomorrow to go over what's wrong with it," she told him.

"Oh, great. Thanks," he said.

Case still wasn't sure how he felt about a small-town guy named Dusty nosing around under the hood of his car, but he couldn't come up with any immediate alternatives. Once again, the conversation moved to territory Case was unfamiliar with, so he spent the next hour sitting on the sofa with his eyes closed, the sound of idle chitchat and gentling rain filling his ears. He was comfortable, slowly relaxing, but he tensed every time Rawley shifted in his chair and brushed their knees together.

Case pretended to nap while the warmth created by the man's deep voice and occasional touches infused him. Eventually Rawley announced his departure. Case listened to the rustling of fabric and soft footfalls as Rawley prepared to leave. He and Aunt Sylvia shared a few last softly spoken words before Case heard the front door open and close. Case remained where he was on the sofa, eyes closed, as he finally relaxed completely with the rumble of the sheriff's departing engine.

That man had Case wound up on a level he'd never experienced before. Case found he loved, hated, and feared it all at the same time. He knew how he would have handled the feeling yesterday, but today was a new start, and he didn't know to act. Aunt Sylvia lightly brushed a hand over his hair as she passed, leaving Case to the quiet of the room as he drifted to sleep.

Chapter Six

IT WAS ONLY Thursday, but it had been a long damn week and Rawley was feeling every second of it. Clover City's crime rate was pretty low, so the majority of calls he and his deputies answered were theft, domestic disturbances, or drunk drivers. Every so often, they would get an influx of drugs, but it never lasted because there wasn't much hardcore drug use here. Those who sought that kind of fix tended to migrate to the big cities where cocaine and heroin were more readily found. Rawley had been a cop in Denver for almost a decade, but he hadn't had a single major crime in the years he'd been here, something for which he was eternally grateful.

Rawley had spent the past four days in his truck with his trusty radar gun, nailing speeders at various points across town. The past two days, he'd been sitting at the railroad crossing at the edge of town; a hot spot for teenagers speeding down the main road and over the tracks without looking. It had been a year since the last death occurred on these tracks and he intended to keep the streak going. He sighed loudly as he tore off the latest ticket and gave the seventeen-year-old boy behind the wheel his usual speech about safety. He'd given out half a dozen the past couple of days, but if it saved a life by making the kids think twice, it was worth the mind-numbing boredom.

Rawley climbed back into his truck, shut off the emergency lights, and drove back to his parking spot partially hidden by the wall of the feed store near the tracks. It had been the usual quiet on the crime front the past several days, which was typically a welcome occurrence for Rawley, but ever since Case Holden's arrival, Rawley's thoughts had been plagued by gray-blue eyes, dark hair, and a perfectly toned body. He spent his nights tossing and turning, imagining Case in any number of different scenarios, every one of them sexual. The whole situation was frustrating him. He took the edge off every night with his hand, but it didn't satisfy the deep need he had for another man's body—Case's body in particular.

Rawley shifted on the bench seat and adjusted himself. He seriously needed to get a grip. The moment Case climbed into his truck, drenched from the rain, Rawley had suspected he was gay, but after running into each other several times around town the past few days, Rawley was now certain. The knowledge only worsened his predicament because he knew if he wanted Case badly enough, he could have him. The man didn't even try to hide his sexuality or his attraction to Rawley. When they'd seen each other the day before at the general store, he'd been wearing a dark-blue T-shirt that had "Out and Proud" stamped across the chest in rainbow lettering.

They'd found themselves face-to-face in front of the dairy display—Rawley in his tan police uniform and Case looking like a model in his skintight T-shirt and painted-on jeans. Conversation had been polite but stilted. Rawley knew it was his fault because he was too busy noticing every little dip and curve of Case's body to speak coherently.

Knowing Case was gay and that he wouldn't make a play for the younger man had Rawley short-tempered and sniping at everyone. That was why he was sitting alone on the outskirts of town, doing traffic duty; no one wanted to be around him, including himself. Rawley stared into the distance, wondering what the hell he'd done in this life or a past one to earn him this level of torture, when a vehicle he would've been hard-pressed to miss caught his attention. The bright-gold Mustang roared past him, registering ten miles per hour over the speed limit.

"Oh, you've got to be shitting me," Rawley muttered. He turned on the emergency lights and siren as he pulled onto the road.

There was only one person in Clover City who drove a Mustang. He caught up to Case quickly, and they pulled to the side of the road, Rawley coming to a stop a few car lengths behind Case. Rawley exited the truck and walked up to the driver's side of the car to find Case had rolled down his window and held out his license and insurance card. Rawley took them, willing his body not to react to the beautiful smile Case offered him. Rawley couldn't help but notice that Case wore a black shirt that made his hair seem even darker and those gray-blue eyes brighter.

"Get pulled over a lot, do you?" Rawley asked, averting his gaze to Case's papers.

"My car tends to draw attention," Case answered. Rawley rolled his eyes at Case's nonchalant shrug.

"Your *car* draws attention," Rawley muttered.

Everything about Case drew attention, or at least Rawley's. He put his mind to the task at hand, making sure Case's license and insurance were up-to-date before handing them back through the window.

"I didn't get pulled over driving my aunt's Jeep."

"Did you speed in the Jeep?"

Case shrugged. "It was a manual with no oomph."

"Slow down," Rawley said as he turned on his heel to return to his truck.

Rawley repeatedly told himself the reason he wasn't issuing Case a citation was because this was his first offense, but it was actually because Case had just gotten the Mustang back from Dusty's garage earlier that day. He didn't want to intrude on Case's newly reclaimed freedom. Rawley wasn't prone to leniency—he would have written up anyone else, first offense or not, but he found it impossible to inhibit Case's happiness...for the time being. If he continued to be reckless, Rawley would write him up.

Rawley heard the Mustang's door open and the resultant dinging, but he refused to turn around. He didn't want or need to see Case in his skintight clothing again; it left very little to the imagination. Despite his intention to not look back, Rawley glanced over his shoulder to find Case's black jeans-clad legs extended outside the car, elbows braced on his knees as their gazes locked and held.

"Are you going to be at the barbecue Saturday?" Case asked, still sitting sideways in his car, watching him.

Rawley nodded as he climbed back into his truck. Once inside the cab, where his arousal couldn't be seen, he allowed himself the luxury of looking Case over, admiring every inch of those long legs, toned forearms, and handsome face. Even at this distance, with glass and metal between them, Rawley could feel the heat of those gorgeous eyes infusing every cell in his body. It took more effort than he cared to acknowledge to pull his gaze away from the tantalizing sight fifty feet in front of him, but he somehow managed it. Rawley scowled at his internal turmoil as he turned off the emergency lights, wondering why Case hadn't gotten back into his car to drive away yet. After a few minutes of staring at each other, Case shook his head, pulled his feet back into the car, and closed the door. Case waved out the window as he drove away down the main road, leaving Rawley feeling aroused, irritable, and, if he were honest with himself, quite a bit lonely.

Chapter Seven

CASE EASED OUT of his aunt's Jeep and looked around at the surrounding farmland currently occupied by dozens of cars. Music drifted on the air from the massive barn, creating an interesting soundtrack for the setting sun. In the distance was a farmhouse that looked to be much smaller than the barn. Aunt Sylvia made her way inside where she was greeted with enthusiastic hugs and warm smiles. Case followed behind more slowly, trying to take in the sights, sounds, and smells that were bombarding him. He'd been to a few city barbecues and a million parties, none of which had come close to what he was currently experiencing. The atmosphere was entirely different, lighter, friendlier, and simply struck him as something more meaningful for some reason.

"Casey, come here. I want to introduce you around," Aunt Sylvia said as she took his arm so she could lead him steadily around the barn. She introduced him to so many people, there was no way he would remember all their names and faces, though he did recognize a few from his trips into town. He remembered Matt and Cameron, two firefighters he'd met while shopping for groceries, and Leland was an EMT who'd approached Case at the movie theater. They'd struck up a conversation that morphed into whispered jokes during corny scenes of the film and the promise to "do it again, sometime."

Eventually, Aunt Sylvia wandered away with a close friend of hers, leaving Case to take up residence at a table situated along the back wall. He liked that spot because he could see everything, so he took a few minutes to relax and enjoy watching the townsfolk interact. It was the epitome of the small-town stereotype where everyone knows everyone, strangers are not to be trusted, and secrets don't exist. The bits and pieces of conversation he could overhear were far more personal than he was accustomed to, making him feel like an unwelcome voyeur. Case's stomach rumbled as he inhaled the delicious scent of fire-grilled meat. He couldn't stop the smile that spread across his face as a mother tried to teach her young son how to dance on the makeshift floor set up in front of the local band playing country music, old and new.

Case felt so much more relaxed and happy at this gathering than he ever had before, and he suspected it was because no one at this party expected anything of him. That thought took him back to the men he'd left behind in Denver. Pulling the cell from his back pocket, he read three more responses to the text he'd sent earlier that morning. Over the past week, it had become clear to Case that simply running away from his problems wasn't going to help. He actually needed to make changes. He knew sending a breakup text was cowardly, but he just didn't have it in him to argue with six men.

After reading the last message, he silenced the phone and tucked it away, choosing to immerse himself in the local culture—something he hoped to become a part of. Aunt Sylvia had happily agreed to Case's request to extend his visit from a few weeks to several months. Several minutes later, Case had the uneasy feeling of being watched and glanced around the room to find Rawley standing by the entrance, staring at him. Their gazes locked for several seconds before Rawley turned away, but Case continued to stare. The man was downright handsome.

Rawley had changed out of the tan sheriff's uniform he typically wore when on duty, and was now wearing fitted jeans with an untucked, green button-down. The shirt's color made Rawley's deep-brown eyes appear lighter, and those jeans were molded to perfectly muscled thighs that made Case sigh in longing. He was blessed with the show-stopping view of a firm round ass when Rawley bent down to hug an elderly woman who barely reached his sternum. Case swallowed roughly as he imagined what Rawley would look like naked, with all that tanned skin pulled tight over well-defined muscles, eyes darkened with desire.

"Casey," his aunt said, startling him from his musings. "I want you to meet Jake and Ryan."

Case pushed the remnant of his daydream aside and stood up to greet the men his aunt had walked over. He had heard his aunt talk about the two on several occasions. He'd made the assumption they were brothers, but seeing them together now, it was obvious they were a couple. Ryan was a good-looking, thirtyish, dark-haired guy with chocolate eyes, where Jake was the exact opposite with blond hair and soft-blue eyes. Case hadn't expected to meet other gay men in town, but he immediately felt more at ease knowing he wasn't the only one. It was clear the townsfolk were comfortable and accepting of the relationship, since this little shindig was taking place on their property. Aunt Sylvia saw another friend enter the barn and excused herself, leaving Case in the awkward position of making conversation with complete strangers.

"How long will you be in town?" Ryan asked.

Case shrugged and slid his thumbs into his pockets. "A week, a year... I deliberately left it open-ended," he said.

"So, what? You just told your boss and landlord you were leaving for who knew how long, just like that?" Jake asked.

"No. I don't have a job and I own my house, so I didn't really have to clear it with anyone. I just packed a bag and left," Case told them.

"How can you afford that sweet ride you drive around town and own a house without a job?" Ryan asked in disbelief.

"Savings," Case answered.

It was a question Case had been asked a million times before, but if he had learned anything over the past week of analyzing his life, it was that telling people you were independently wealthy brought out the users and abusers. When he thought back to the six men he'd been "dating," he saw that pattern as clear as day. One or more of the men would call him, ply him with alcohol and attention, and then fuck him until they inevitably got what they wanted because Case wanted to feel like he was needed. It became a revolving door of men who had initially made him feel loved, desirable; six men had wanted to be with him, after all, but he must have known what was going on in the back of his mind because he'd felt miserable, empty, and lonely. It was depressing that it had taken Aunt Sylvia's offer of a visit and his subsequent road trip to make him see the situation for what it was—use and habit. Case practically broke out in hives when he thought about going back to that life, so he'd made himself a promise. When he did go back, things would be different.

"So, you guys work this farm?" Case asked.

Both men nodded. "Corn on one side. Alfalfa on the other. Jake also helps out at the post office several days a week," Ryan answered. Case nodded, holding Ryan's gaze for a moment before glancing at Jake.

"I feel awkward asking, but," Case said, wondering how his next question would be received, "what's it like here for you? You know, being a gay couple."

"Pretty much the same as it was in the city. You get people like all the ones here tonight who are great, but there are homophobic assholes, too. Last year someone painted obscenities on the side of the barn and told us 'fags' to go back where we came from." Ryan shrugged.

"I've never lived anywhere else, so..." Jake said, mimicking Ryan's shrug and smiling.

"How did you guys meet? I mean, if you're a city boy like me, and he's always lived here..." Case asked, genuinely curious. Ryan shifted on his feet, apparently uncomfortable, while Jake fell into a fit of laughter.

"Oh, well, see, he hit me with his truck—" Jake said.

"I didn't hit *you* with the truck, I hit the tractor. And only because you pulled out onto the road in front of me," Ryan interrupted.

"Whatever. He broke both my legs—"

"I didn't break both legs. It was a hairline in your shin and a barely noticeable crack in your ankle, and that was from you freaking out and jumping off the tractor, not from the impact of me running into it. Jesus, Jake, you're making it sound worse than it was," Ryan said, exasperated.

Case laughed at the couple as a smiling Jake slid his arm around Ryan's waist. Ryan reciprocated the act by wrapping a beefy arm around Jake's shoulders and kissing his temple.

"Anyway"—Jake said with a roll of his eyes — "I knew it was an accident and didn't want to press charges, but Kane wasn't going to just let it go so he made Ryan do what he called community service, which was basically living with me and helping on the farm until I healed enough to do it myself. Ryan was all grumpy about it at first, but I was like, hell, yes! I mean, do you see this face?"

Jake kissed Ryan's blushing jaw, and Case couldn't help but laugh. These two men were obviously completely in love, and it did funny things to Case's heart, knowing that Rawley was the catalyst for their relationship forming. Thinking about the man had Case searching the barn until he once again found Rawley standing amidst a group of men, two of them in the tan police uniforms. One of the officers was talking, gesturing animatedly, and the group was laughing at whatever was being said. Case swallowed convulsively at the sight of Rawley smiling.

He soaked in the vision, because every other time he found himself in Rawley's company, the man had a scowl on his face and spoke as little as possible. There was a time or two when Rawley's gaze had been heated, almost lustful, but it would quickly be hidden behind a cold, indifferent stare, which led Case to believe that while the man liked Case's appearance, he didn't really like *Case*. Or maybe Rawley was just a straight man who didn't know how to handle finding another male attractive.

"Is he gay or not?" Case heard himself ask out loud, causing Jake and Ryan to look over their shoulders.

"Who?" Jake asked when they turned back. Ryan just raised his eyebrows in question when Case glanced at them.

"Um..." Case's mouth went dry. He wasn't sure this was something he should be discussing. Rawley was Clover City's sheriff, and Case didn't want to make him the focus of the small-town gossip mill. "Will you keep it to yourselves?"

They both nodded.

"The sheriff," he said.

The men's dual reactions confused Case. "Someone has eyes for the sheriff," Jake cooed, smiling and waggling his eyebrows.

Case shook his head, but couldn't hide his smile or blush.

"No one knows for sure, but occasionally he gives off vibes. Know what I mean?" Ryan said.

Case knew firsthand what Ryan meant, and the mixed signals Rawley put out were messing with his head. "Sometimes I think he's checking me out, but most of the time, I'm pretty sure he hates me," Case admitted.

The three men discussed Rawley and all his oddities for a few minutes before the conversation branched off to other topics. Case was amazed at how easy it was to talk to the couple, like the three of them had been friends for years. The band struck up a lively song that Jake swore was his all-time favorite as he pulled Case onto the wooden-plank dance floor. Case had never danced to country music before but found the moves and company to be energetic and fun.

After several songs where he danced first with Jake and then Ryan, he excused himself to get some fresh air. Case walked outside to the side of the barn, holding his hands behind his head so the nighttime air could cool his overheated body. He hadn't realized how hot it was inside. He looked up at the night sky dotted with stars. That was something he never saw in the city with the lights obliterating the view. Out here in the country with only the light from the moon, the stars were clearly visible.

He frequently sat on the back steps of Aunt Sylvia's house late at night just looking up at them. His mind and body were still on the nightlife partying schedule, so going to sleep before midnight was a rare occurrence.

Case's mind was lazily wandering over his life in the city and the multiple phone calls he'd been receiving from his past lovers, all wanting to know when he'd be back. Every single one of them had disregarded the text he'd sent stating he was done with that life and he was moving on. Case was taken by surprise when strong arms wrapped around his waist as a hard body pressed against his back. He was moved forward until his chest was pressed to the rough wood wall of the barn, and Case placed his palms against it. Case could feel the man's arousal poking him in the ass. He was prepared to resist the unwelcome attention, but his plan to fight changed immediately upon hearing the deep voice that accompanied the body.

"You feel as good as you look," Rawley said gruffly, voice low as he held Case against his chest. "You're so fucking hot."

Rawley's rumbling voice and close proximity made Case shiver, the sheriff's actions completely unexpected. Surreal. Rawley buried his face between Case's neck and shoulder as he tightened his grip around Case's waist. His other hand skated across Case's chest to his arm where Rawley gripped his biceps. Case rested his forehead against the barn and lowered his arms but kept his hands firmly planted against the wall. He didn't know what was happening and thought it best to let Rawley control the interaction. When Rawley rubbed his erection over Case's ass, Case decided to break the silence.

"You're pretty hot yourself, Sheriff, but what are you doing?" Case asked and involuntarily pressed back against Rawley's crotch. Rawley removed his hand from Case's biceps to cover his mouth.

"Don't talk," Rawley demanded, barely above a whisper.

"Okay," Case mumbled against Rawley's hand. The desire to stick his tongue out to taste Rawley's skin was intense, but Case managed to check that urge.

"I need to think," Rawley said.

Rawley rested his forehead on Case's shoulder. Case reached up to smooth his palm over Rawley's hair until he encountered the skin of Rawley's neck, and then he gently massaged the muscles there. He leaned against Rawley's body and used his other hand to pry the fingers from his mouth. Case lowered Rawley's hand to his chest, simply enjoying being held by the man. He let his head fall back onto Rawley's shoulder so he could look up at the stars. It felt good to be embraced like this by a man who didn't have an ulterior motive for doing it, at least not a currently obvious one. Case had no idea what had spurred Rawley into suddenly coming on to him, but he wasn't about to complain. He was too excited at finally knowing the sheriff was gay and that the attraction he felt was mutual.

Chapter Eight

RAWLEY WAS AFRAID to move, afraid to even breathe. He couldn't believe he had Case in his arms. He had acted on instinct, not thinking his actions or the potential repercussions through. If he *had* thought about what he was doing, he never would have done it. Rational thought had left his brain the minute he'd seen Case dancing with Jake and Ryan. The couple had effortlessly drawn Case out of his self-imposed isolation so Rawley got to see a little of the party boy he was rumored to be. He hadn't been able to tear his eyes away from a carefree and happy Case Holden. When Case wandered outside, Rawley had immediately followed.

Now, outside in the dark, with Case's firm body pressed to his in all the right places, Rawley found it difficult to think straight. All he knew was that if he followed his desire all the way to the bedroom, he would feel shitty when Case returned home. Rawley felt damn vulnerable, and he hated it. For the thousandth time in his life, Rawley wished he was the kind of guy who could have meaningless sex, but he wasn't. His heart always got involved and he inevitably ended up hurt.

"Nothing has to happen," Case said softly, as though reading Rawley's tumultuous thoughts, or perhaps he was just good at picking up on physical cues—like Rawley's tense muscles and shallow breathing.

Rawley lifted his head and put his chin to Case's shoulder. He took a deep breath of cool air, which did nothing to abate the heat pulsing through his veins, and let it out slowly. He wanted nothing more than to take this hot rod home, to lose himself inside his sweet young body for the night. Rawley let out a resigned sigh and pulled away from Case, instantly missing his heat and strength. Case turned to face him.

"I'm hungry," Case said, stepping into Rawley's space, their body heat once again mingling. "Let's go back inside, get some food, and just spend some time together."

Rawley's heart rate picked up at that suggestion. He'd let his attraction and desire be known to Case, but he certainly wasn't ready for the rest of the town to know. As if once again reading Rawley's thoughts, Case attempted to put him at ease.

"It isn't unusual or suspicious, is it? Just two guys eating and talking. There's nothing to worry about. Do you think twice about being seen with Ryan or Jake?"

Rawley immediately felt foolish. Case was right. He had no idea why he was suddenly concerned that everyone would know he was gay just because he sat at a table with Case at the town's annual barbecue. He didn't even know why it would matter if they did and then began to wonder if he'd be successful at keeping his interactions with Case platonic. He cleared his throat and stepped back, creating some much-needed distance.

"No, you're right. Never gave it any thought at all."

Case nodded in the moonlight and brushed Rawley's arm as he passed, heading back into the barn. Rawley followed more slowly, trying to regain control of his mind and his body's reactions. Someday Clover City would know they had a gay sheriff, but Rawley wasn't ready for it to be today. He re-entered the barn to find Case had waited for him just inside the door. Case smiled when Rawley came to a stop beside him.

The interior of the barn was buzzing with activity, and Rawley's gaze automatically scanned the gathering for problems. Everyone seemed to be enjoying themselves. No drunken brawls had broken out like last year. At least, not yet, but the night was young. Last year's fight was the reason he had two deputies in uniform working here tonight.

Rawley followed behind Case, trying hard not to notice the way his ass moved as he sidestepped down the buffet table, loading his plate with roasted vegetables and a small amount of hickory-glazed turkey. Apparently, he had been saving room on his plate for dessert because he placed a slice of chocolate cake and a cream cheese danish on a second plastic plate. Case shot Rawley a huge grin as he grabbed napkins and two plastic forks. Rawley's own plate was heaped high with chicken wings drenched in honey barbecue sauce, chips with artichoke dip, a spoonful of beans, and a rather large helping of potato salad. With plates in hand and bottles of beer tucked under their arms, they headed toward the barn's entrance.

"Do you mind if we eat outside? It's nice out and I love looking at the stars," Case said.

Rawley nodded his agreement. He was all for getting Case alone and being able to speak freely.

"That's something you don't see in the city," Case added.

"I know. It was one of the first things I noticed after moving here," Rawley said.

"Yeah, Aunt Sylvia told me you were from Denver. So am I. She told me you moved here after being injured in the line of duty."

Case rounded the back of the barn and sat on the ground, leaning against the wall. He kicked his feet out in front of him and rested his plates on his lap as he pushed his beer bottle into the dirt so it wouldn't fall over. Rawley sighed as he joined Case on the ground, mimicking his position. He was slightly annoyed that Sylvia had told all that to Case, but he wasn't surprised. He'd been the topic of small-town gossip the moment he'd run for sheriff. Rawley had managed to keep the intimate details of his life out of the public eye, but the shooting was part of his employment file, and therefore taken into account by town officials, especially when it became clear he was going to win the bid for sheriff.

Conversation was halted for several minutes while they ate. Rawley noticed Case's eyes rarely strayed from the sky. He seemed relaxed and content just sitting in silence, stargazing, listening to the sounds of the night around him. Rawley didn't want to ruin the moment by speaking, but he had to clear the air and make sure Case was on the same page with him. When he finally spoke, he kept his voice low and his tone soft.

"I'm sorry I came at you like that. It was...um." Rawley had been about to say it was unprofessional, but that wasn't the correct word. All he knew was that he should have approached Case differently, like maybe not at all. "It was impulsive," he finished when Case rolled his head against the barn wall to look at him with lustful eyes.

"Yeah. You surprised me," Case admitted.

Rawley's own lust spiked as Case smiled at him and rubbed the toe of his shoe along Rawley's ankle. The hole in his heart left by his previous boyfriend made his chest ache with longing. He desperately wanted that spot filled, but he was terrified of losing someone else. Case continued the gentle caress as he turned his attention back to the star-sprinkled sky. Rawley couldn't tear his gaze away as Case took a swallow of beer, the movement of his lips and throat captivating him. Loneliness, sharper and stronger than ever before, exploded in Rawley's veins. Suddenly all he could think about was wrapping himself around Case, being inside him, and chasing the cold away with the combined heat of their desires.

"I don't know you," Rawley whispered into the stillness of the night, watching Case's expression carefully for any sign that his words were unwelcome. "But I want you." The dull, rapid thump from the music inside mimicked Rawley's heartbeat at the admission.

Case laughed softly. "Up until a week ago, it never mattered to me whether I knew someone or not. If we found each other attractive, we'd fuck. Didn't matter to me where or even how."

"I'm the exact opposite. I've always cared...how, when, where, who. Shit, I even cared why. I wanted to know it all and understand it. Makes me a great cop, but a horrible boyfriend."

"I can see that. If it were me and I was all fired up to be naked with you, and you started questioning me about it? Yeah, I'd probably just move on to someone easier and more willing."

"Are you telling me you're not interested?" Rawley asked. On the surface, he wanted Case to reject him. Deep down, where the war was waged, Rawley wanted Case to accept him and everything he was offering.

"Oh, I'm interested. I've got a boner just thinking about us together, but I'm trying to be...better? More mindful? I don't know. All I know is that I'm failing, and the longer we sit here, the more I want to drop my pants and beg you to fuck me."

The battle inside Rawley escalated. It seemed his libido and the years of loneliness and celibacy were winning. His self-preservation and the fear telling him to be cautious became white noise in the background as he pushed to his feet. He picked up his trash and empty beer bottle as Case did the same. They walked in silence to the front of the barn where they disposed of their dinner plates, placing the bottles in the recycle bin. Rawley waved to an elderly couple as they exited the barn, heading for their car. He looked back to find Case staring at him with unconcealed longing. He imagined his face looked much the same, which meant they had to get away from the town gathering. Anyone with half a brain would be able to see what was going on between them.

Rawley held Case's gaze as he snagged his hand, turned, and pulled Case toward his truck. He knew Case hadn't driven himself because the Mustang was nowhere in sight, and he wouldn't have known where the McKesson Farm was located. Rawley had parked the truck on the gravel shoulder of the road a good distance away, just in case he got called in. He couldn't have his truck blocked by dozens of other parked cars should an emergency arise, even though the likelihood was low.

The night was quiet except for the muted country music spilling out the open front doors of the barn and the crunching of their shoes against gravel. Rawley opened the passenger door for Case, who rubbed against him slightly as he climbed inside. He closed the door and walked around the front of the truck quickly because now that he'd made the decision to be with Case, he was in a hurry to get him home and naked. Rawley jerked the truck onto the road, aiming it toward town as Case pulled out his phone. He glanced at Rawley with the cell pressed to his ear, waiting for the other party to pick up.

"Hey. Just wanted to let you know I left, so you wouldn't be looking for me," Case said once his call connected. After a moment, he added, "No, I feel fine. I was just ready to leave. Don't freak out if I'm not home when you get there... Okay...night."

Case's gaze raked over Rawley's entire body as he disconnected the call and Rawley felt the look like a physical touch. Damn. If Case's eyes could cause that kind of heat to spread through Rawley's body, what would it be like when they were finally skin-to-skin? When Rawley was buried deep inside him? A bolt of lust shot straight into his dick and he shifted on the seat uncomfortably.

Case tucked his phone back into his pocket, the movement awkward due to the seat belt, before reaching over to caress Rawley's tight fist on the steering wheel.

"Relax. There's nothing to worry about. Nothing has to happen," Case said.

Rawley made a conscious effort to loosen his grip on the wheel. "Maybe no worry for you, but it's been over two years for me," Rawley said. "I'm about to explode over here."

Case moved his hand from Rawley's fist to his thigh and squeezed. "Pull over."

"Case, please," Rawley said.

"Just pull over," Case urged softly.

Rawley pulled the truck to the side of the road and put it in park. He left the engine running as he turned toward Case. Case clicked open his seat belt and leaned across the bench seat. The kiss he gifted Rawley began as a soft brush of lips before growing bolder. Rawley sucked Case's lower lip into his mouth, nipping at it gently as he slid his arm around Case's back in an attempt to pull him closer. He wanted to feel that toned warmth pressed against him again.

Case positioned his body on the seat so that he could kiss Rawley and slide a hand down to palm Rawley's erection. Case gripped the shaft, pumping his hand against the zipper and causing the most intense friction Rawley had ever experienced. Case explored his mouth with his tongue, helping push Rawley's desire to a fever pitch. No one had ever touched him like this before. Not once in his entire life had Rawley ever had a man draped across his lap, tongue in his mouth, hand on his cock while sitting in a vehicle on the side of the road where anyone could see.

A thrill spiked through him at the knowledge that he was about to take part in something he was constantly ticketing teenagers for. Rawley massaged Case's back while he gripped Case's wrist to slow the movements on his dick. He didn't want to come in his pants. That would be both messy and embarrassing. Case eased the pressure before completely breaking contact to shut the truck's engine off. Rawley's groaned complaint earned him another soft kiss, a lustful gaze through lowered lids, and a naughty smile.

"Let me taste you," Case mumbled against Rawley's mouth as he lowered the zipper to pull Rawley's cock through the opening.

Case kissed him again, hard, shoving his tongue past Rawley's lips as his thumb swiped across the pearl of precum on the tip of his dick. Needing more freedom, Rawley unbuttoned his jeans, lifted his hips, and pushed his pants down just far enough to release the entirety of his cock. Case immediately wrapped strong fingers around him and Rawley jerked as a jolt of pleasure shot through him. He had denied himself to the point that he was balanced on a razor's edge. All it would take was a few hard strokes from Case and Rawley would explode in his hand.

Case broke the kiss, scooted his butt across the seat, leaned over Rawley's lap, and engulfed the entire length of his penis at once. The crown hit the back of Case's throat, making Rawley wonder at the lack of hesitation or hint of gag reflex. It was obvious in this moment that Case had a lot more experience than Rawley initially imagined. Rawley let out a strangled cry as he fisted a handful of Case's silky dark hair.

Case's tight lips and hot mouth combined with Rawley's years-long dry spell had his fingers digging into Case's scalp, holding him in place as Rawley thrust into his mouth. He wanted the moment to last, but at this stage, he was incapable of stopping his orgasm from barreling down on him. What felt like only seconds later, Rawley grunted, gasping to get enough oxygen into his lungs, as his body stiffened. He came in a rush of expelled breath and semen, hips jerking with each spasm. His dick convulsed as Case sucked harder, apparently determined to pull every last drop of Rawley's cream down his throat.

Case let Rawley's softening cock slip from between his lips before sitting up and licking his lips. He smiled broadly as Rawley fought to catch his breath. Rawley's entire body relaxed into postorgasmic bliss, and he rested his head against the cool glass of the rear windshield. He grabbed Case by the back of the neck so he could pull him in for a slow, tongue-filled kiss. He had never kissed a man after that man had given him a blow job, but he found the taste of himself on Case's tongue to be intoxicating. Too soon, Case broke away and turned the ignition, bringing the truck to life with a grumbling roar. Rawley pulled his pants up and tucked himself away, amazed to find he was still half-hard. He should have been limp as a noodle after a blow job like that, even if he had only lasted seconds.

"Maybe now you can relax and focus a little better," Case said as he buckled his seat belt.

Rawley couldn't help but laugh at that. He had certainly been on edge. He was far less anxious than he had been, but he found he was still impatient to get Case home. Fifteen minutes later, they arrived at Rawley's house, which was situated in the middle of an old, well-kept neighborhood where the houses were small and the yards even smaller. It was a two-bedroom ranch-style brick home with yellow shutters and a green lawn that needed to be mowed after all the rain that had fallen. He parked in the one-car driveway that was barely wide enough for the truck, and both men climbed out. Case followed him to the door where he patiently waited for Rawley to unlock the deadbolt. Rawley stepped aside to allow Case to enter the living room ahead of him. He walked in after, turned on the lamp nearby, and then locked the door behind him.

Case stood in the center of the living room, looking around. Rawley's breath caught in his chest as he watched the beautiful young man in his private space. He thought back over the years since he'd moved to Clover City, trying to remember the last time he'd had company, but came up empty. Case turned with a smile, causing his brain to completely fizzle out. Rawley pulled Case to him, crushing their bodies together before pressing their mouths together in a bruising kiss.

Case was in his house, the bed literally mere feet away, just around the corner, which made Rawley become insane with impatience and need. He held Case with a hand to the back of his head as he squeezed his butt cheek with the other, pressing their bodies together and grinding their erections against each other. Case snaked his arms around Rawley's waist. His hands brushed lightly over Rawley's ass before he slid them under Rawley's shirt, igniting tiny fires everywhere he touched.

Case had already seen him, tasted him, and Rawley shuddered at the memory of the incredible experience. But he was feeling cheated and concerned that Case would change his mind, so he moved quickly. He broke the kiss to yank Case's shirt over his head and then dropped it to the floor so he could work on opening Case's jeans. Case wrapped strong fingers around Rawley's wrists to still his frantic, uncoordinated movements. Rawley responded by hooking fingers through belt loops and pulling Case in for another kiss. Case ran his palms over Rawley's forearms, up to his biceps, and then back to his wrists. Holding firm, Case moved backward slowly, one step at a time, tugging Rawley along with him.

"Bedroom's this way?" Case asked as he continued moving toward the short hall.

Rawley nodded as he released the belt loops in favor of holding Case's ass in his hands and pressed their chests together, using his body to guide Case in the right direction. He marveled at how Case fit against him perfectly, being only an inch or so shorter than Rawley. Rawley had never experienced this kind of frantic lust with anyone other than his last boyfriend, and he was becoming increasingly desperate. He ignored the little voice in his head that reminded him desire had never overridden his brain, or his self-preservation, even with Alex. Case's calm, unhurried actions irritated him, and he started to wonder if the blow job on the side of the road had been enough for Case. Rawley maneuvered Case around the corner into the bedroom and pushed him onto the bed.

The room was dark except for the light spilling in from the living room, but it spotlighted Case's semi-prone form on the bed in the most flattering way. The only way the vision could be better was if he was naked. Rawley stared for a moment before he began to undress. Case stood up. He opened his jeans, pushed them down over his hips and legs before sitting on the edge of the mattress to finish removing them. Case was all smooth, pale skin stretched over toned muscle, and his thick cock stood at attention between his legs. A light dusting of dark hair covered his chest, tapering down to offer a nice backdrop to his swollen length. Rawley's mouth went dry as a drop of moisture glistened in the slit, and he licked his lips as he imagined taking it into his mouth. Rawley's feet moved him closer to the bed, seemingly of their own accord. His gaze never strayed from an aroused, naked Case, reclining on the bed, waiting for him.

"You're amazingly handsome," Case whispered.

"Me? Have you looked in a mirror?" Rawley asked as he knelt on the floor between Case's splayed legs.

He wrapped his fingers around Case's hard shaft, stroked it a few times, and then took it into his mouth, sliding all the way down until his nose was buried in the hair surrounding it. He gagged slightly, pulled back, and then went down again, inhaling Case's scent. Case threaded his fingers through Rawley's hair and threw his head back with a gasp as Rawley worked him to a fever pitch.

Rawley disengaged from Case's hold, grabbed Case's hips, and lifted him farther onto the bed. It had been a long time since he'd had a man in his mouth, but as much as he loved the taste of Case on his tongue, he wanted—needed—to be inside his body more. Case scooted until he was in the middle of the mattress, Rawley following close behind. Once Case was comfortable, Rawley spread Case's legs and settled on his stomach between them, taking that delicious cock back into his mouth. He delighted in the reaction caused by brushing his fingers over Case's pucker.

The light, teasing sensation made Case's body twitch and his ass clench in anticipation. Rawley brought his fingers to his mouth, wetting them enough that he could slide them inside Case with ease. Case gasped with the initial entry, gripping Rawley's finger with that tight muscle, but then moaned and relaxed when Rawley sucked his cock back into his mouth, teasing the underside of his dick with his tongue as he pumped and twisted his fingers inside Case's hot, silken passage.

"Shit," Case gasped as Rawley introduced a third finger.

Case raised his knees, spread his legs wider around Rawley's shoulders, and dug his heels into the mattress. He bounced his hips, fucking Rawley's mouth and fingers with abandon. Rawley relaxed his jaw, allowing Case to shove deep into his mouth, only to drive his ass down onto Rawley's fingers with every hip bump. The sight of Case's unrestrained arousal and confidence to take what he needed pushed

Rawley to the edge; his dick throbbed with the need to release. Case's spine arched as his ass clenched around Rawley's fingers spasmodically, and Rawley knew he was close, too. He pulled back, allowing Case to slip from his mouth, but he kept his fingers buried inside the warm, silken channel. He planted lazy kisses along Case's quivering thigh muscles and at the creases of his knees as Case recovered. His body relaxed, the sweet little hole opening farther for Rawley.

Rawley took immense delight in how quickly he brought Case close to orgasm. He decided to do it again, only this time, he would watch as his lover tumbled over the edge. He engulfed Case's cock in one fluid motion, hollowing his cheeks and sucking hard as he flexed his fingers inside Case. He pressed against that magic spot repeatedly once he found it. It didn't take long before Case lifted to one elbow, fisted Rawley's hair, and yelled as his pleasure poured over Rawley's tongue. Case flopped to his back, gasping in ragged breaths when Rawley released his softening dick and pulled his fingers free.

He didn't want to give Case too much time to recover, though, so he jumped off the bed to grab a condom and lube from the nearby dresser drawer. He returned to kneel between Case's legs. He held Case's hooded gaze as he rolled the condom down his painfully hard shaft and slicked it. Rawley fisted the base of his cock to stave off his own orgasm as he positioned the head at Case's entrance and pushed it gently into the fluttering hole. He stopped after the tip popped in and slid his forearms under Case's knees as he leaned over to brush a light kiss on Case's chin. He covered Case's mouth with his, swallowing Case's surprised gasp when he shoved the entirety of his thick shaft into him with one long, slow thrust. He looked into Case's eyes, trying to find any indication that he was causing pain, but only saw a mirror of his own raw desire swimming in the smoky blues.

His hips came to rest against Case's upturned ass, his dick surrounded by incredible heat as he bottomed out. Case clamped down on him when Rawley adjusted on top of him; the movement almost had Rawley coming right then. He brought the intensity down by kissing Case softly and slowly, using his tongue to explore the depths of Case's mouth. Rawley had done what he could with his fingers to prepare Case to take him, but damn, the boy was tight. Absolutely perfect. Rawley smiled when Case began touching him, smoothing his hands over Rawley's face, down to his neck, his chest, and then around to his back. Those hands never remained in one place for long.

"You feel incredible," Case said breathlessly.

"So do you. So fucking hot and tight around me," Rawley said before biting at Case's lower lip.

"Yeah, please, Rawley. Now. Fuck me," Case pleaded, rocking forward as he grabbed Rawley's thighs on either side of his hips and squeezed.

Rawley didn't need to be asked twice. He pulled back until he was just about to pop out and then snapped forward, driving into Case hard.

"Oh, yeah," Case whispered as Rawley did it again, increasing the pace with each inward push. Sweat beaded on their skin as they both strained for release.

"I'm close. Don't stop. Don't stop." Case wrapped his fingers around his cock and began stroking himself furiously to the rhythm of Rawley's hammering thrusts. He clenched his teeth as he arched off the bed. Seconds later, he erupted, painting his body with ribbons of come.

Rawley was spellbound by the beauty of Case in orgasm. The sight had his balls pulling up and his cock swelling. The intensity of the sensations bombarding him lifted him to his knees. He buried himself deep inside Case and roared as he filled the condom. When he was completely empty, Rawley rested back onto his heels and brought Case's ankles to his shoulders. He rubbed his hands over the bones of Case's ankles, over his lightly furred calves to his muscled thighs, while they both struggled to catch their breath. After a moment, Case slid his legs down Rawley's arms to the mattress, and Rawley reluctantly pulled free of Case's warmth.

"Damn," Case whispered.

"Yeah," Rawley grunted as he rolled off the bed. He removed the condom as he walked across the hall to the bathroom, tossed it in the trash, and grabbed a washcloth. He smiled broadly, his ego boosted, when he returned to the bedroom to find Case hadn't moved an inch. Rawley used the cloth to clean Case's chest and stomach and then gave Case's leg a playful swat.

"Under the covers. I'll be right back," Rawley said, returning to the bathroom to attend to his own cleaning.

Chapter Nine

RAWLEY JOLTED AWAKE and lurched into a sitting position, trying to catch his breath, having just relived Alex's death once again in his dreams. He gradually became aware of his surroundings, noting he was in his bedroom in Clover City, alive and well; not lying in a growing pool of his own blood on a cold, dirt-encrusted sidewalk in Denver. It had been months since he last had this particular nightmare. He wasn't sure what brought it on. The bed shifted and a warm body pressed against his back, fully bringing him back to the present. Shit! The disorientation that followed his nightmares had made him forget Case was in bed with him. Rawley scrubbed both hands down his face to wipe the residual images of the dream from his eyes and groaned, knowing the young man at his back was the reason he'd had the nightmare.

"You okay?" Case asked around a yawn as he gently rubbed the tight muscles of Rawley's back.

Case brushed his lips across Rawley's neck just below his ear and then rested his chin on Rawley's shoulder. The warmth of Case's body pressed against his slowly eased the cold tension that had latched onto him during the nightmare, his presence aiding with the physical pain, but it only made the mental anguish worse. Guilt, helplessness, and sadness washed over him as he fought the urge to pull away from Case.

After the shooting when he'd been injured and his partner had been killed, Rawley had been required to see a psychiatrist. Dr. Emmett Rodgers had done his best; Rawley was certain of that, but every so often, he would be overwhelmed with old memories and emotions. Dr. Rodgers had told him he was suffering from PTSD with a little survivor's guilt thrown in, and had stressed repeatedly that Rawley deserved to live his life, to be happy. Six months later, Rawley resigned from the police department and moved away from Denver. He had been running, he knew that, but how was he supposed to be happy in his life without the man he had loved? The man he had called partner both at work and home? Rawley often wondered how Dr. Rodgers's advice would have differed had he known Rawley and Alex had been lovers, but he'd kept that information to himself.

"I'm going to take a shower," Rawley said. "Go back to sleep."

He felt raw. Exposed. Hot tears pricked the backs of his eyes, and suddenly he had to get away. He threw the blankets off and got out of bed, brushing Case's hands aside, his touch too much to take at the moment. Rawley entered the bathroom where he locked the door behind him before switching on the light and starting the shower. While he waited for the water to heat, he looked at his reflection in the mirror. He examined the scar on his left shoulder, where one bullet had gone completely through, and then moved down to his left hip where the second bullet had fractured his pelvic bone. Both spots burned in remembered pain.

Rawley turned away when the mirror steamed over. He adjusted the water temperature and stepped into the shower, finally allowing the tears to fall. It had been just over two years since the shooting, but the pain of loss could still bring him to his knees. Rawley had taken two bullets, but just one had robbed Alex of his life. The unfairness of that made Rawley shake with anger. In the other room, sleeping in Rawley's bed, was another source of guilt. Case was the first man since Alex that Rawley had found remotely attractive, and he was certainly the first to incite thought-stealing lust. Rawley considered himself a broken man incapable of loving anyone other than Alex. Case deserved to be with someone who could love him, commit to him, and protect him.

Rawley washed away the tears and memories, letting the water run over his head until it cooled. He shut the water off and dried himself while trying to make his thoughts agree with his feelings. His head wanted him to remember Alex forever, to never replace him. His heart wanted him to grab onto Casey Holden and never let go. Rawley still wasn't certain which way he would go even as he climbed back into bed with Case.

Chapter Ten

CASE LAY ON his back, staring up at the shadows on the ceiling created by a shaft of dim moonlight shining through the crack in the curtains, and listened to the shower run. He was surprised by how quiet Rawley's neighborhood was. Case had never been aware of the background noise the city made until he had come here where all the stores closed up at six and everyone slept through the night. There were no sirens, no screaming neighbors or barking dogs, nothing for him to focus on other than his turbulent, uncomfortable thoughts. He wanted to know who Alex was but was afraid to ask. Rawley had woken him when he screamed Alex's name, brokenly begging him to stay. Case had only meant to soothe when he'd lightly touched Rawley's arm, but the man had jolted awake. Case was jealous that just hours after making love to him, Rawley would dream about another man, even though that jealousy made no sense. Rawley wasn't his...yet. Case also found that he didn't like the idea of Rawley hurting and the desire to comfort his man was strong.

The water turned off and Case rolled to his side, facing away from the door. Rawley had pulled away emotionally as well as physically, and Case was debating on whether or not he should leave before the man came back, but that internal conversation died a quick death when he remembered he wasn't in the city where a ride home was a phone call away. If he wanted to go home, Rawley would have to take him. A few minutes later, the mattress dipped behind him as Rawley climbed back into bed. Case wanted to go back to sleep, but Rawley's breathing was shallow and rough, telling Case he was still hurting.

"Are you okay? Should I leave?" Case asked softly.

Several moments of uncomfortable silence followed in which Case struggled to keep his own breathing normal. Depression and anger made his chest feel tight as he considered the possibility that he'd reverted to his old ways of having sex with a man because the man wanted it, and now, having gotten what he wanted, Rawley was casting him aside. Case fisted the sheet at his stomach. He'd thought Rawley was different, that what they had shared was different, but maybe he'd been wrong.

"Shit," Rawley whispered.

The bed shook as Rawley changed position, wrapping a strong arm around Case's stomach, spooning up behind him. Rawley nuzzled Case's hair and then kissed him softly on the back of his neck.

"I'll be fine. Don't pull away," Rawley murmured against his skin.

"I'm not the one who pulled away," Case said.

"Casey..." Rawley groaned, pressed his lips more firmly against Case's neck, and tightening his hold.

"No one calls me Casey except my parents and sometimes Aunt Sylvia." Though Case had to admit he liked hearing Rawley say his name.

"I won't use it anywhere but here, like this," Rawley told him. He moved his hand over Case's chest and then up to lightly grasp the base of his throat. He put a leg over Case's waist, pulling Case tightly against him in a full-body embrace.

"What's wrong? You're acting odd," Case asked, lightly stroking his fingers over Rawley's forearm.

"I'm so damn cold," Rawley whispered into his ear. "And you're so warm. I can't get close enough."

"Actually, you can't get any closer." Case grinned in the darkness as Rawley adjusted against him, raining kisses over Case's neck and shoulder. "Rawley?"

"Yes," he whispered as he dragged his lips over the shell of Case's ear.

"Who is Alex?"

Rawley froze. He released Case's earlobe from his lips before burying his face between Case's neck and the pillow. Rawley tightened his arms around Case as he sobbed, breaking Case's heart a little at the pain this strong, protective man was suffering. He pulled Rawley's arms away just enough to allow him to roll over and card his fingers through Rawley's hair soothingly.

RAWLEY COULDN'T STOP the fresh flow of tears. The memories of Alex were still too close to the surface, even with Case in his arms, rubbing his head and neck. Case had taken him by surprise by asking about Alex. Rawley must have yelled his name during his nightmare because that was the only way Case would know about him. What else had Rawley said before he'd jolted awake? Rawley adjusted on the pillow so he could look at Case in the semi-dark room. A shaft of moonlight that managed to squeak past the heavy curtains cast Case in shadow and outlined him with a soft glow. His fingers never stopped their gentle motions on the back of Rawley's head.

"Alex is...was..." Damn. Rawley choked just saying his name, and he had no idea where to even begin, what to say. So many memories flooded his brain, vying for his attention, each bringing with it a wave of intense emotion.

"I'm sorry. You don't have to answer. It obviously hurts you," Case said as he placed a soft kiss to Rawley's chin.

"It does hurt, but I don't know why. It's been over two years," Rawley said. He slid his palm over the smooth skin of Case's back while still holding him close. He felt cold to his bones, and Case felt hot in comparison. He wanted as much of Case's body pressed against him as he could manage.

"You love him."

"Loved. He's dead," Rawley whispered. It was the first time he'd actually said those words out loud, and he couldn't put any real volume behind them.

"You don't stop loving someone just because they die, Rawley. You loved him then, you love him now, you will continue to love him for the rest of your life."

Rawley closed his eyes as Case kissed along his jaw, his words soothing Rawley's heart, relieving the pressure a bit. Case moved his hand from Rawley's neck to his shoulder. He pushed, rolling Rawley to his back and draping across his chest—a living, breathing blanket of heat. Case framed Rawley's face with both hands and stared down at him.

"I'm so envious and jealous. You had one man who captured your heart completely. Me? I had six men back home, and I don't love any of them. And I'm damned sure they don't love me, no matter what they say when they orgasm. At best, they can be classified as fuck buddies—sex toys with monetary needs." Case tensed in Rawley's arms for a moment and then took a deep breath before relaxing again. "God, I hated my life," Case whispered.

Rawley moved a hand down over Case's lower back to his butt, slipping a finger between the cheeks to press against his hole while holding Case against his chest with an arm around his waist. Rawley lifted his head to take Case's bottom lip into his mouth. Case threaded his fingers through Rawley's hair and pulled his head back to expose his throat where Case nipped at his Adam's apple before moving down to the hollow of his throat. Case's ass clenched around the tip of Rawley's finger as he pushed it in.

CASE ROLLED HIS hips and they both groaned with the pleasure of their cocks sliding against each other, but this was as far as Case was willing to go at the moment. He wanted Rawley inside him again, but the timing felt wrong. They'd both just reopened wounds, although the death of a loved one far outweighed Case's pathetic boyfriend problem, but neither of them was in the right frame of mind for sex. Case had had enough of using sex as a diversion and feeling like he'd been used as such.

Rawley needed reassurance, empathy, and comfort. Case found he was more than willing to give all that, and more, for this man, but he wouldn't allow himself to be a distraction. Case kissed Rawley's neck, his jaw, gradually working his way up to his lips before he slowly rolled off Rawley. The action pulled Rawley's finger from his ass, but Rawley didn't object; he simply turned with Case and wrapped both arms around him, holding him tightly.

"Will you tell me about it?" Rawley asked as he once again tried to climb into Case's skin.

"About what?" Case asked around a yawn. Now that Case knew who Alex was, he was more comfortable with things between him and Rawley; he relaxed, ready to go back to sleep. The steady rise and fall of Rawley's chest against Case's back as he breathed, and their combined warmth, was making Case drowsy to the point he was having a hard time staying awake.

"Your life, how you came to have six boyfriends, why you're in Clover City with me instead of home with one of them...everything," Rawley answered around a huge yawn of his own. "I don't want to be one of seven, Casey."

Rawley's yawn sparked another one from Case that threatened to crack his jaw. "You're not," Case assured him as he drifted off to sleep surrounded by the warmth and comfort of Rawley's embrace.

Chapter Eleven

RAWLEY WOKE TO an unfamiliar ringing. It took a moment for his sleep-fogged brain to realize it was Case's phone. He reached a hand out to wake Case only to find he was alone in the bed before he noticed the shower was on in the bathroom. He rolled to the side of the bed and looked at the floor, trying to locate the phone. The ringing seemed to be coming from Case's jeans near the foot of the bed. Rawley yanked the jeans off the floor and patted them down until he found the phone stuffed into the back pocket. Once he could see the display, he read Sylvia's name. Rawley considered letting it go to voicemail for a heartbeat before the cop in him took over. What if she was hurt or something happened to a family member and Case needed to go home? He was pressing the accept button before he could reconsider.

"Is everything okay, Sylvia?" Rawley asked, all business.

"Well, it was. Has something happened to Casey? Why do you have his phone?" Sylvia rushed out, her concern evident with every word, and Rawley realized his mistake.

"No. I mean, yes, he's fine. I didn't mean to scare you. He's in the shower. I answered because I saw your number and thought something had happened and you needed him."

Rawley clamped his mouth shut because, first, he was rambling. Second, it had just occurred to him that he'd answered Case's phone at six-thirty in the morning. If Sylvia had wondered where Case had spent the night, she had her answer. Rawley raked a hand through his hair and squeezed his eyes closed. He and Case hadn't taken the time last night to discuss how they would move forward without all of Clover finding out or even if they were going to see each other again. Rawley wanted more than a one-night stand, but knowing what he did now of Case's city life, he wasn't sure Case felt the same.

Sylvia's soft laughter filtered through the phone. "I can almost hear you blushing, young man. I give you my blessing, but let me tell you something," she said more sternly. "You had better guard that boy's heart like the treasure it is. He's been through enough over the past years with men who just used him for sex and money."

Rawley couldn't fault the woman for the warning, but it angered him just the same. "I am not using him, Sylvia. Not for sex and not for money. I brought him home last night because I had to be with him. I couldn't stand another minute not knowing what it felt like to hold him or kiss him. He's the most beautiful and vibrant man I've ever met," he said with more vehemence than he'd expected.

Rawley replayed his words, but decided he wouldn't change a single one. Case was young, beautiful, and energetic, which was the polar opposite of Alex, who had been ruggedly handsome, bulkier in build, and older. Rawley had loved Alex deeply, but Alex was dead, and for the first time since being shot, Rawley felt alive. Case was responsible for that, for making him feel again. Of course, most of the past week, since Case had arrived in town, Rawley had spent his time frustrated and aroused, but at least he was feeling *something*. Rawley scrubbed a hand down his face with a groan.

"I am so up shit creek when he goes home," Rawley mumbled to himself, but Sylvia heard.

"Then I suggest you don't let him leave. There's nothing there for him anymore," she said.

Rawley folded his legs beneath him on the bed and propped his elbow on his knee, rubbing his forehead. He stared at the star-patterned quilt while a million questions about Case and his life in Denver filled his head. Sylvia said there was nothing there for him, but from their short conversation last night and the gossip mill around town, it appeared Case had everything to go back for.

"Well, I just wanted to check on him. Make sure he was okay. He didn't tell me where he was going last night when he called. Now that I know he's with you, I'll stop worrying," Sylvia said.

"Okay," Rawley mumbled. It was the best he could do with all the other stuff whipping through his brain, not the least of which was the fact he had just outed himself to a prominent member of the town's social committee.

"Maybe I'll see you later when you bring him home," Sylvia said, and Rawley could hear the happiness behind the words as she disconnected the call.

Rawley straightened his legs and flopped onto his back with a groan. He adored Sylvia, but she was a talker and her circle of friends were the town gossipers. It would be only a matter of hours before his sexuality became the topic of discussion. News that the sheriff was gay was sure to spread through town like a tsunami. He rolled his head on the pillow as Case came flying into the room and jumped onto the bed, landing on top of him.

Rawley clenched his legs together and brought his knees up, deflecting Case's weight up toward his stomach rather than allowing him to land on sensitive parts. Case laughed as Rawley rolled him across his body to the opposite side of the bed. Once the minor disaster had been averted, Rawley relaxed, allowing Case to climb back on top of him, straddling his hips. The young man was beautifully naked, his dark hair still damp, trails of water snaking over the skin of his neck and shoulders. Rawley thumbed a drop of water just below Case's ear as Case ran his palms over Rawley's bare chest.

"So, you're answering my phone now?" Case asked as he gently pinched Rawley's nipples.

"Yes, I'm sorry, but I saw Sylvia's name and thought something might have happened. She was just worrying about you, though," Rawley answered.

He stroked his thumb across Case's earlobe before dragging his fingers down Case's neck and over his chest to his thigh, loving the contrast of toned muscle beneath smooth skin. Rawley resented the barrier the sheet and quilt created between their bodies, but he wasn't quite ready for Case to get off of him. Rawley loved Case's weight on him, his scent, his touch, and his incredible warmth. Case shifted his weight down Rawley's legs so he could lie across his chest, propping his chin in the palm of his hand and looking into Rawley's eyes.

Rawley sighed in contentment as Case got comfortable on top of him. Once the wiggling stopped, Rawley slid his hands around to cup Case's firm, round butt cheeks. He didn't want to let this man go. The urge to cuff him to the bed frame so he could never leave was strong enough to have him eyeing the handcuffs holstered to his utility belt on top of the dresser. Unaware of the direction Rawley's thoughts had gone, Case smiled down at him and lightly scratched at his pecs.

"I was going to ask you how you wanted to play this, since it seems no one in Clover knows you're gay, but now I'm confused. You answered my phone so Aunt Sylvia knows I stayed the night with you, which means half the town will know by lunchtime. I can't figure you out. Were you closeted or not?" Case asked, lightly tracing Rawley's jawline with a fingertip.

"Depends on your definition of closeted. Have I announced to everyone that I'm gay? No, but I don't deny that I am. There's just never been a reason for me to say anything."

"Well, I guess we could spin it to work for you. I came over, we watched a game, and I fell asleep on the sofa, or something like that."

Case's tone was light, but his expression was troubled. His boy didn't like the idea of being denied, even if he had been the one to suggest it, and Rawley was delighted that Case didn't want to hide the fact they were seeing each other. Having crossed his own line in regards to the handsome young man, he didn't want to deny them, either, but public opinion about his sexuality or their age difference was a problem for him. He couldn't be seen as the gay sheriff who used his position to coerce wounded young men into his bed. Casey Holden wouldn't strike most people as a victim, but Rawley had a strong suspicion he had been mistreated in the past.

"We're not doing that," Rawley said as he gripped Case's ass, pulling him upward for a kiss.

When Case opened his lips, Rawley slipped his tongue inside, tasting the slightest hint of mint toothpaste and something that was distinctively Case. Rawley swallowed Case's groan. He squeezed his butt cheeks as Case began grinding their erections together. He reluctantly released his hold on Case's ass to wrap his arms around his back and roll them, placing Case beneath him, covered by the blankets. The cold air on his bare ass triggered his bladder, and he growled against Case's mouth before breaking the kiss.

"Sorry. I've got to pee." Rawley nipped Case's lower lip before pushing off.

"Romantic." Case laughed.

Rawley stood by as Case stretched his arms toward the headboard to lengthen that lithe, sexy body. Rawley's already uncomfortable morning wood twitched at the sight. Case noticed and threw the covers off his body to grab his own erect cock. He lowered his lids, moaning low in his chest as he stroked his shaft with deliberate slowness. Rawley's gaze locked onto those long, thin fingers where they squeezed, released, stroked, and twisted.

"Better hurry, Sheriff, before I come without you," Case said, peering up at him with hooded eyes.

That beautiful face, those gray-blue eyes so clearly filled with lust, nearly did Rawley in. Rawley spun on his heel and hurried to the bathroom. The sight of Case masturbating on his bed would forever be burned into his memory with such clarity he would no doubt be using that perfect picture on future lonely nights. While in the bathroom, Rawley splashed water on his face, swished a little mouthwash, and ran a comb through his hair. Replaying Case's hand moving over his dick slowly progressed to other, more erotic images, like Case sinking that gorgeous thick cock into him.

He palmed his own hardening dick. His ass clenched as he imagined taking Case deep inside him. Rawley was traditionally a top, and he'd only bottomed once years before when Alex wanted to explore, but neither one had really enjoyed the position reversal and had resumed their usual roles. So why, suddenly, could he not stop thinking about Case topping him? In fact, the more he thought about it, the more he wanted it. Pushing aside all his concerns over his sexuality becoming common knowledge and their age difference being the topic of hair salon gossip, he returned to the bedroom with single-minded purpose.

He found Case still on his back in a nest of rumpled sheets with his ebbing erection lying on his thigh. Despite the threat of coming alone, Case was waiting for Rawley, and as soon as he saw him reenter the room, his cock surged back to life.

Chapter Twelve

CASE SMILED, OUTRIGHT ogling Rawley as he stepped back into the room. Damn, but his cop was hot, with damp brown hair spiked on his head, laugh lines around his eyes, and sexy lips set into a firm line. He let his gaze drift over the man's tanned, muscular body, zeroing in on the bulbous head of his erect cock. The man was seriously aroused. Rawley strode toward the bed with such determination that Case knew he was seconds away from another good pounding. He couldn't wait. He got onto his hands and knees at the edge of the bed to present his ass to the gorgeous older man. Case sucked in a breath and bit his bottom lip when Rawley grabbed his hips, sank his teeth into a butt cheek, no doubt leaving a mark. He straightened with an open-handed smack to the other cheek.

"Do you want to top, Casey?"

Rawley pulled Case off the bed by his hips. Once on his feet, Rawley pressed against his back, embracing him from behind while reaching one hand down to stroke his engorged cock. Case eased his head back to rest on Rawley's shoulder with a sigh.

"Because I want you inside me," Rawley whispered into his ear just as he gave the dick held loosely in his fingers a firm tug.

Case pulled Rawley's teasing hand away and turned to face him, threading his fingers through Rawley's hair. He took Rawley's lips in a possessive kiss while turning them so Rawley's back was to the bed. Case had topped a few times before, but definitely preferred being the bottom because he loved the feeling of being stretched and filled—dominated— by his partner. There was something intriguing about having this big, strong cop beneath him, begging to be fucked, that he couldn't deny. Case broke the kiss, pressed his palms to Rawley's chest and pushed, eager to feel the older man's ass clenched around him. Case was toned, but he wasn't the strongest person in the world. He smiled when Rawley went down on the mattress without hesitation, legs spread in invitation.

"I want you on your hands and knees, handsome," Case said. Rawley immediately complied.

A nudge to the back of the thighs was enough to signal Rawley to move farther onto the bed so Case had room to climb onto the mattress behind him and settle between his spread calves. Case slid his fingers between perfectly rounded globes to pull them apart so he was able to see Rawley's taint clenching in anticipation. Rawley opened his legs farther and lowered his head to the mattress. His balls hung high and tight, thick cock pointing toward his head. Case fell in love with the sight. He smiled as he licked a path across Rawley's scrotum, up over his perineum to his pucker, where Case drew patterns with his tongue. Rimming was one of his favorite things, both to give and receive, and it did amazing things to him having a strong man like Sheriff Rawley Kane offering up his ass like this. Determined to give this powerful man a fucking he wouldn't soon forget, Case stiffened his tongue and speared Rawley's hole.

RAWLEY JERKED IN surprise when Case pushed his tongue into him. He had never been rimmed before, had never even considered it since no man he'd ever been with had suggested it. Not even Alex had done more than plant a kiss on his butt cheek or the back of his thigh every so often, and Rawley was thoroughly enjoying having Case do something so intimate. A text popped up on the screen of Case's cell phone that effectively killed Rawley's arousal and enjoyment.

The words had only been visible momentarily before the screen blacked out again, but it had been long enough for Rawley to read it. It hadn't been anything overtly personal, but it had reminded Rawley of Case's current situation. The man had six boyfriends waiting for him in Denver, for fuck's sake. Rawley surged forward, away from Case's incredible-feeling tongue, and lowered to his stomach to roll off the bed. Case sat back on his heels to stare at Rawley in confusion, face flushed, eyes glittering with desire. Rawley hated putting a stop to their lovemaking during such an intimate moment, but he couldn't enjoy himself with the shadows of six men suddenly hovering over them. He tossed the offending phone to Case, who didn't even try to catch it. He let it land on the bed between his knees, never breaking eye contact with Rawley.

"I won't be number seven. I can't be," Rawley told him.

He'd said it the night before, but it was important and bore repeating. The words came out calm and steady, but Rawley felt completely out of control, which was not the norm for him. Intense desire for the boy warred with depression over the knowledge he wasn't entirely available, with quite a bit of jealousy that he wasn't the only one in Case's life. It surprised him to realize how much he wanted to be with the guy, just not while six other men were still in the picture. Rawley mentally kicked himself for starting something that might well have nowhere to go, because one day, Case would return to Denver.

Rawley grabbed a pair of jeans off the chair by the door on his way out of the bedroom. He needed a little space and a few minutes away from Case to get his emotions under control so went into the kitchen to put some coffee on, pulling his pants on as he made his way through the living room. He hoped Case took the time alone to text his boyfriend back. *I miss you. Come home.* Simple words but strong enough to make Rawley want to scream in frustration. Rawley was standing at the counter, watching the coffee brew, lost in thought, when Case pressed his hot, young body against Rawley's back and hugged him around the waist.

"You're not number seven, Rawley. You're the only one," Case murmured into his ear.

He desperately wanted to believe that, wanted to relax into Case's warm embrace, to enjoy their time together, but his damn brain was back in control and wouldn't allow it. He sighed heavily.

"Am I? When you go back to Denver, whose bed will you fall into first?" Rawley's tone was sharper, more accusatory than he'd intended, and Case stiffened a bit behind him. He hadn't even meant to ask which man Case would go to because he didn't want to know, but it was out there now. He couldn't take it back. After a moment, Case relaxed again and tightened his arms around Rawley's waist, pressing a kiss to the back of Rawley's neck before answering.

"My own. The whole point of this trip was to get away from them, the life they were a part of, and to figure out what I wanted to do to change things. It would be pretty stupid to go back and fall into the same routine."

Case kissed the indent where Rawley's neck and shoulder met before releasing him. He hadn't realized he was cold until Case's heat was gone, and he missed it immediately. Rawley turned around to face him and gripped the counter behind him when he noticed Case was still naked. How had he not suspected that when he'd felt Case's bare chest pressed against his own bare skin?

So many different urges assaulted him as Case casually leaned against the sink across from him. He wanted to reach out and pull Case back against him so he could soak in his warmth and feel his soft skin. He wanted to ask him if he missed the city or if he preferred the small-town atmosphere of Clover City. He wanted to know if Case would consider moving to Clover City in the future, but that was a dangerous line of thinking. The fact he was even having such thoughts made Rawley freeze with shock. When the hell had he started falling for Casey Holden? Rawley swallowed hard and averted his gaze to the living room visible over Case's shoulder.

"Would you like breakfast before I take you home?" Rawley asked, his throat raw.

Case smiled at him lazily. "That would be great."

"Go get dressed. I'll scramble up some eggs," Rawley said. He reluctantly turned his back on the splendid naked vision standing in his kitchen to pour himself a cup of caffeinated bliss and start breakfast.

Chapter Thirteen

CASE LEFT RAWLEY in the kitchen and returned to the bedroom to get dressed. One second, he had been enjoying the feel of Rawley, anticipating the moment he would sink into the handsome man's body, and the next, Rawley was pulling away. Unsatisfied need coursed through his veins. He briefly entertained the idea of stroking one off, but then remembered his phone on the bed where he'd dropped it after checking the text message that had abruptly ended their amorous activities.

He'd immediately followed Rawley to the kitchen in an attempt to put the man at ease. He had every right to be angry. Garrett had chosen a horrible time to contact him, and Case hadn't thought about his phone being where Rawley could easily read any incoming messages. How was he supposed to think about trivial things like his phone and ex-boyfriends when he had Rawley naked and waiting for him? It really was too much to ask.

Case picked up the phone and shoved it into the back pocket of his jeans. He would have to deal with Garrett and the others sooner rather than later, but not right now. He was with Rawley, in Rawley's home, and he was the only man Case wanted. Over the past week, four of Case's ex-lovers had either called or texted him, all saying the same thing— *I miss you. When are you coming home?* A bellowed curse followed by a loud crash sent Case running back into the kitchen.

"What happened? Are you okay?" Case asked, his heart beating wildly in his chest.

Rawley gripped the edge of the stove tightly, with his chin tucked to his chest, which was expanding regularly as Rawley took deliberate, measured breaths. Case could practically feel the anger rolling off him. A skillet of burned eggs sat in the sink behind Rawley. Case wasn't sure if Rawley would accept being touched right now, so he shoved his hands into his pockets and waited, even though the swells and valleys of

Rawley's back presented one hell of a temptation. It was hard to keep his hands to himself. He wondered how Rawley would respond if Case dragged his tongue up the length of his spine. After a moment, Rawley released his grip and straightened, slowly turning to look at Case. His fury, and the struggle not to unleash it, was written in the hard lines of his face.

"Rawley…" Case started but stopped because he didn't know what to say. He didn't even know what had happened in the few minutes he'd been gone to make Rawley so angry.

"Why do you have six boyfriends, Casey? How does something like that happen?" Rawley asked loudly.

"Had, past tense," Case corrected. "And honestly, I liked the variety. I didn't set out to have six men; it just happened because I never said no. Besides, I wouldn't call them boyfriends, really. They were just men I enjoyed fucking. I felt sexy and desirable having six men want me, but eventually, only recently really, I figured out that they only came around, only wanted me, when they needed something, usually money. When I heard Parker tell one of his friends that if he needed cash he should just fuck me and I'd give it to him, I decided things needed to change."

Case stopped talking when he realized how pathetic he must sound. It was one thing to know his life was shit, but quite another to admit to the man he was falling for that he'd been stupid and naïve. Painful embarrassment that he'd allowed himself to be used in such a way burned his cheeks and made it hard to breathe. He averted his gaze, afraid Rawley's expression would be one of pity or worse, disgust, and changed the focus of the conversation to the burned eggs.

"Why are the eggs burned?" he asked.

"I wasn't paying attention. Happens when you're around," Rawley answered.

His voice was softer, the hard edge gone, and Case didn't know what to make of that. He also wasn't sure how to feel about being told he was a distraction. Was that a good thing? Case propped a hip against the counter and stared at his feet. Rawley closed the distance between them, took Case into his arms, and pressed a kiss to his forehead.

"That wasn't an insult. I haven't been able to think straight since you climbed into my truck a week ago, soaked to the bone and beautiful." Rawley buried his nose in the hair on top of Case's head. "Can't stop thinking about you and everything I want to do with you, but then I remember how young you are, or something happens to remind me that you're only visiting, that I'm setting myself up for heartache. I can't take the back and forth anymore, Casey. It's making me cranky."

Case lifted his gaze to look into Rawley's eyes, relieved to see open honesty. It was sad to think how rarely he got to see that in a lover's eyes. He pulled his hands free of his pockets and rubbed Rawley's bare skin, from his belly to his chest and then up to his neck, where he cupped the tense muscles at the base of Rawley's skull. Case brushed his thumbs over the rough stubble at his hairline behind his ears.

"I have no reason to leave."

In fact, the man holding him right then was one of the main reasons he would stay. Case wouldn't tell Rawley just yet how much power he wielded over Case's decision to stay or go. It was too soon. Plus, Case was still concerned that he would fall into his usual pattern of mistaking lust and mutual sexual release for love.

"Not yet, maybe. But I don't want to start something with you only to have you leave tomorrow because one of your fuck buddies figured out the right thing to say to make you go back."

Rawley's tone took on a hard edge, his eyes sparking with barely contained anger, and Case wondered how much of Rawley's current state was due to Case's history and how much was the result of their interrupted session in bed. Case was certainly on edge from not finishing. Rawley released Case and stomped out of the kitchen, leaving Case to stare at the wall in confusion. Rawley clearly had abandonment issues, probably brought on by Alex's death, especially if it had been unexpected. Before he could change his mind, Case followed Rawley into the bedroom. His phone vibrated in his pocket as he entered the bedroom and he cursed under his breath. Rawley cast a glance over his shoulder as he finished buttoning his shirt and then began tucking it into his slacks. Case had hoped they'd get to spend the day together, hiking or simply driving through the countryside, but that dream fizzled at the sight of Rawley's tan uniform.

"You work today?" Case asked, unable to mask the disappointment he felt.

Rawley nodded as he exhaled a sigh. "I don't go in for another hour or so, but I need to feed you and drive you home. Finish getting dressed. We'll hit a diner in town for breakfast. I just destroyed the only food I had in the house."

"I thought we could spend the day together when I agreed to breakfast, but you have to work so you can just take me straight home. I can feed myself."

Case pulled his shirt on, hunted down his socks, and then sat on the edge of the bed to put his shoes on. His phone vibrated a second and third time in rapid succession so he yanked it out of his back pocket to see who was so insistent. He was prepared for messages from Garrett or one the others but not his aunt, and he was instantly concerned when he saw she had called twice. Her text message was simple.

CALL ME.

"I'm taking you to breakfast, Casey," Rawley said firmly. His back was to Case, so he didn't see Case's worried expression. Case hit redial and stared at Rawley's backside as the man secured his utility belt around his waist.

"Hold that thought," Case said while he waited for his aunt to answer. The moment the call connected and he heard her voice, he blurted, "What's wrong?"

"You have a visitor here. He showed up a few minutes ago, claiming to be your boyfriend," Sylvia answered.

Case closed his eyes and rubbed his forehead. "Who?"

"Jordan."

Case let out a pained groan. What the hell was Jordan doing there? Case hadn't told any of his exes where he was going, only that he was visiting family.

Case pinched the bridge of his nose and mumbled a heartfelt "shit."

Rawley startled him by sliding his fingers through Case's hair. Hearing that Jordan was at his aunt's waiting for him had given him tunnel vision so he'd momentarily forgotten he was in Rawley's house, sitting on Rawley's bed. He looked into the sheriff's eyes, drawing comfort from Rawley's gentle touch.

"I'll be home soon," Case told his aunt and then disconnected the call.

"You're pale," Rawley said as he gently massaged the back of Case's head with his fingers. "What happened?"

Case swallowed hard as he shook his head, unsure how to tell Rawley one of his ex-lovers was waiting for him.

"Nothing bad, just inconvenient and unwanted, but I do need to get home. Raincheck on breakfast?"

Rawley nodded, his concern over Case's distress clearly written on his face. Case didn't bother to untie his shoes. He just yanked them onto his feet, ignoring the fact they were a bit loose. His only thought was getting back to his aunt's and sending Jordan home to Denver.

Chapter Fourteen

RAWLEY DROVE CASE home in silence, frequently stealing glances at him from the corner of his eye. Case stared out the side window, but Rawley doubted he was watching the scenery. Since the phone conversation in the bedroom, Case seemed to be lost in thought and unable to focus. The only reason Rawley wasn't going all cop in this situation was because, despite whatever was happening at home, Case was calm. Rawley had tried asking a few questions to figure out what was going on, but Case had been tight-lipped and vague. He didn't know Case all that well yet, but the young man wore his emotions on his face for all to see, so if something truly bad was going down, Case wouldn't be this composed.

Rawley's gaze was once again pulled to his companion when Case rolled his shoulders and neck to ease the obvious tension in his muscles. His posture had become increasingly rigid the closer they got to their destination. Rawley reached over to place his hand on top of Case's where it rested on his thigh. Without turning away from the window, Case rolled his hand to thread their fingers together and squeezed. Rawley brought their joined hands to his lips and kissed Case's smooth knuckles. He reluctantly released Case's hand, placing it on his thigh when he turned the truck down Sylvia's drive, needing both hands on the wheel to keep the vehicle from veering off the rutted road.

How Case had managed to get his Mustang down this driveway was a mystery. The man would have to drive slower than a snail to avoid slamming the undercarriage onto the rocks and packed dirt with every dip in the uneven ground. Rawley would have to talk to Ted about getting this road graded and leveled, maybe even paved, so Case wouldn't have to worry about damaging his car. Any shock that might have resulted from planning the future as though Case would be a part of it was immediately forgotten when he pulled to a stop behind a sleek black Corvette covered in dust. Rawley decided there was a hidden road onto Sylvia's property he didn't know about that allowed these fancy cars access.

Case stiffened and his grip on Rawley's thigh tightened. Rawley's attention was drawn from the handsome man beside him to the expensively dressed pretty boy lounging on the front porch with Sylvia. Sylvia looked at them apologetically as anger and sadness battled for dominance in Rawley's chest. This was exactly what he'd been worried about when he'd wrapped his arms around Case outside the barn the night before, and the possibility he'd chosen to ignore when he'd taken him home to his bed. The heat of Case's hand on his leg bled through his uniform pants, contrasting sharply with the cold he now felt. Rawley bit back his many questions—Who was this guy? Why was he here? Was Casey happy to see him? Case's strained features suggested he wasn't overjoyed by the unannounced visit.

Case removed his hand from Rawley's thigh with a heavy sigh so he could climb out of the truck. Glaring daggers at the gorgeous, smiling twink on the porch and hating everything he represented, Rawley turned the truck's engine off. He stayed only a short distance away as he followed Case onto the porch. The last thing he wanted to hear was a reunion between Case and one of his lovers, but the jealousy bristling under his skin pushed him to stake his claim so lover boy would know Case was no longer available. Unfortunately, that idea died quickly.

Chapter Fifteen

CASE WALKED TO the porch, not really wanting to have the conversation he knew was coming. He glanced over his shoulder to see Rawley was following. When Rawley had spotted Jordan sitting next to Aunt Sylvia on the porch, his posture had become rigid and his jaw hardened. If looks could kill, Jordan would have burned to ashes where he sat. The hard-ass cop Case had become accustomed to seeing, the cop he was hopelessly attracted to, was back in all his stunning glory. Jordan's soft laughter reached Case's ears as he trudged up the three steps to the landing.

"Got yourself arrested again already?" Jordan asked, eyeing Rawley as he stopped a few feet away.

Case had forgotten Jordan's boyish face and scrawny build. He much preferred the strong, authoritative masculinity of the older man standing behind him. The two couldn't be more different. Rawley was solid muscle, a day's worth of stubble across his jaw, with eyes that had seen too much ugliness and a wounded heart. The gun and handcuffs only added to his overall sexiness. Jordan was way too thin, shaved himself smooth everywhere, and was obsessed with his looks and keeping up appearances.

Having Rawley and Jordan in such close proximity to each other, Case couldn't remember what it was about Jordan that had attracted him. Their relationship felt like a distant memory, even though he had just seen Jordan eight days before. So much had changed since then, most of it taking place deep inside Case, forever altering his heart and mind.

Rawley crossed his arms over his chest, averting his eyes as Jordan engulfed Case in boney arms. Case, on the other hand, kept his gaze on Rawley as he grabbed Jordan by the hips and pushed him away. He didn't want any affection from Jordan, or anyone else, while he had the sheriff in his life. Rawley was the only one Case needed. No longer did he need six men to fill the void. Sheriff Rawley Kane was man enough to fill it all by himself, and Case loved that.

Jordan didn't catch on to the fact Case was trying to extricate himself from the hug and cupped Case's face in his hands to hold him still as he licked along the seam of Case's lips. He opened his mouth to tell Jordan to stop and immediately regretted it. Jordan took Case's mouth in a tongue-filled kiss that made Case's stomach knot. It felt so wrong. The only man who should kiss him or touch him in such an intimate way was Rawley.

After several seconds, Jordan finally noticed that Case wasn't reciprocating and was in fact trying to get away so he stepped back, breaking the kiss. Aunt Sylvia was stepping into the house, staring over Case's shoulder, and he couldn't sense Rawley anymore. The metallic thud of a car door closing made Case spin on his heel to see Rawley behind the wheel of his truck, bringing the engine to life. Their gazes locked long enough for Case to mouth *I'm sorry* before Rawley squared his jaw, threw the truck in reverse, and backed up enough to turn around. Case watched with a heavy heart as the man he wanted more than anything disappeared down the road in an angry cloud of flying dirt and rocks.

They hadn't looked at each other long, but Case had seen the expression on Rawley's face. He didn't know if it was anger, hurt, or regret, but he damn well knew he never wanted to see it again. He placed his hands on the railing and bowed his head, fighting down an anger of his own that had been building up for years. Jordan's horribly timed and unwelcome visit was threatening to push him to the breaking point. Maybe that's what it was going to take to drive home the fact he was done with these men—erupting into a fit of anger and lashing out.

Either unaware or uncaring of Case's tumultuous emotional state, Jordan slid his arms around his waist, pressing his chest snugly against Case's back. Case straightened at the erection prodding him in the ass. This was not happening. Case roughly extricated himself from Jordan's embrace, which wasn't hard to do given how thin the guy was. Nothing at all like Rawley's powerful arms. Without a word or glance, Case entered the house and felt Jordan follow, close on his heels.

"What the hell is wrong with you?" Jordan demanded. "Every other time I've surprised you like this, we were naked and fucking like rabbits inside of five minutes."

Case scanned the living room and kitchen in one quick sweeping glance to ensure his aunt hadn't heard Jordan's words, pleased to find she was elsewhere in the house.

"Watch what you say around here," Case hissed. He stopped in the center of the living room, took a deep breath to steady himself, and then turned to face Jordan. "Where are you staying?" *So I can avoid you.*

"What do you mean, where am I staying? With you," Jordan answered, his tone suggesting it should have been obvious.

"Oh, I don't think so," Case said, shaking his head.

He pulled his phone from his back pocket and stared at it, finger hovering over the screen. It was intriguing the first person he would think to call for hotel options would be Rawley, instead of the woman sitting in the next room. Case tucked the phone back in his pocket with a huff because he didn't have Rawley's number. Something he planned to change the moment he saw Rawley again. He could always get it from his aunt, but he wanted Rawley to be the one to give it to him. Rawley had to make that choice. Case figured his aunt was in the study where she liked to sit in front of the fireplace and read.

"Why can't I stay with you?" Jordan asked. Case didn't remember hearing the whine in Jordan's voice before, perhaps because he'd always gotten what he wanted, but the tone irritated Case just as much as the man's presence did.

"This is my aunt's house, and I'm imposing on her enough. She doesn't need you, too. Wait out here," Case said when Jordan tried to follow him into the study.

Case closed the door in Jordan's face. He turned to find his aunt in her favorite armchair by the fire, right where he expected. She had the TV turned to a soap opera, the volume low, while she thumbed through a gardening magazine. She smiled at him and he returned it, albeit sadly.

"You're okay?" she asked softly.

"Yes and no," Case answered. He was pleased she seemed to understand what he wasn't saying. "I can't make him go home, but he sure isn't staying here. What's the hotel farthest away from here? Besides the Hilton in downtown Denver," Case added with a chuckle. Aunt Sylvia shook her head at his pathetic joke and gave him the name of a fairly cheap hotel in town.

"Thanks," he said, kissing her on the cheek.

Case made Jordan retrieve his overnight bag from his room where Jordan had placed it upon arrival before shoving the man out the door to his Corvette. Case got into the passenger seat and gave Jordan directions to the hotel. He rolled his eyes at all the complaints about dirt roads and small towns, purposefully ignoring every sexual innuendo Jordan threw his way. It was exhausting. It would have been less taxing to fuck the guy, give him some money, and send him on his way.

That's all the damn man wanted anyway—a stiff dick in his ass and cash in his wallet. But that road led to one place—a dead end—and Case was tired of finding himself there. He'd made some significant changes in the past week and he was not going to take a backward slide. The road to the hotel passed in front of the police station, and Case spotted Rawley's truck in the lot, the sight making his heart thump against his ribs. He smiled as warmth spread through his body just at the thought of Rawley. Case was already half in love with Sheriff Rawley Kane and hoped the sheriff felt the same, but he wondered how far back Jordan's little display had set them.

Case's thoughts were interrupted when Jordan pulled into the parking lot of the Cloverleaf Hotel, a squat two-story building with a covered entryway that looked like every other small-town hotel in the country. The hotel was within sight of the police station, making Case wonder if that had been deliberate on Aunt Sylvia's part. They exited the Corvette and Jordan walked into the hotel office with purpose. Case followed more slowly, his gaze impulsively drawn to the police station with the hopes he would catch a glimpse of his man right up until he entered the hotel lobby and his line of sight was obstructed. Jordan stood at the registration counter waiting for Case, smiling flirtatiously at the cute kid behind the desk.

"Did you get registered?" Case asked as he approached.

"Yes, but I wasn't prepared for a hotel expense," Jordan said. He cast an annoyed glare at Case before returning his attention to the clerk, offering an overly sweet smile that made the kid blush.

Case pushed down a wave of irritation as he handed the clerk his debit card. "You drive a Corvette, but you can't afford a sixty-dollar hotel room. You should really think on that while you're here."

Jordan puffed out his chest as he straightened. "I can afford it. I just didn't bring any money with me because I didn't expect my boyfriend to kick me out of his bed."

"It's not *my* bed and we are *not* boyfriends," Case corrected.

The clerk finished ringing up the room and handed Case his debit card and receipt. He crumpled it in his fist when he saw the total. Jordan had booked the room for two weeks, so while the man was out of his aunt's house, he wasn't out of Case's life. The kid winked as he handed Jordan the room key, and then blushed furiously when Jordan responded with an air kiss. Deciding he'd seen enough of Jordan's sexualized antics and wanting to be rid of his company, Case turned to leave. He had just pushed open the glass door, immediately seeking out Rawley's truck, when Jordan caught him by the arm.

"Where are you going?" Jordan asked. "I drove all night to see you. I've missed you and I want to be with you."

Jordan's tone was soft as silk, and his words dripped honey. It once worked like a charm on Case, but not anymore. He didn't want soft or sweet. He wanted harsh truth and whisker burn. Jordan placed a palm over Case's chest, circling a finger suggestively over his nipple in a way that had always been guaranteed to excite him. It still might if the finger caressing him belonged to the right man, but it didn't, so Case roughly brushed the touch away.

"Not going to happen," Case said, stepping outside into the rapidly heating air that would soon make the cool early morning temperatures a sweet memory.

"Case," Jordan called from the sidewalk behind him. He had come out the door, but he wasn't following Case as he strode across the parking lot.

"You drove all night. I'm sure you're tired. Go to the room and get some sleep."

"You're really not coming to bed with me?" Jordan asked, his surprise evident.

"No. I told you we were over last week and I've got things to do." *Like soothe my lover's ruffled feathers.*

Not looking back to see whether Jordan followed his instructions, and not really caring either way, Case crossed the street toward the police station. The morning was quiet, most of Clover City sleeping off the excess food, drink, and dancing of the previous night. Since no one aside from business owners and their employees were up, he hoped Rawley would take the time to drive him home for a second time. As he stepped off the pavement of the road to start across the gravel lot of the station, the door of the building opened and Rawley stepped out.

Chapter Sixteen

RAWLEY WAS AT the hood of his truck before he noticed Case practically standing in front of him. He swiveled his head from side to side, with drawn brows, probably trying to figure out how Case had gotten there, until his gaze focused in on Jordan's black Corvette in the hotel parking lot and he schooled his features to reflect cold distance. Case stepped into Rawley's personal space when he opened the truck door to get in. He plastered himself against Rawley's back, wrapping his arms tightly around the hard body he'd spent all of the previous night loving on. Rawley stiffened in his arms, and Case immediately understood his mistake. He shouldn't have embraced Rawley in public, especially not in front of the police station, but the move had been made and he didn't regret it. He couldn't make himself let go, anyway.

"Don't, please," Case said, his lips brushing over the shell of Rawley's ear.

"Don't, what?" Rawley ground out.

Case kissed Rawley's clenched jaw, feeling the muscles bunch and release beneath his lips. "Don't shut down. Don't hate me. Don't leave me." Case pressed his mouth to Rawley's hot, prickly skin even as Rawley latched onto his wrists to pry open his arms. Case fought the action, not wanting to let go, but Rawley's strength won and he stepped from Case's embrace.

"Please," Case whispered when Rawley released his grip and faced him. They stood toe to toe, close enough to feel the warmth of the other, but not touching. The combination of physical proximity and emotional distance was almost more than Case could handle. It hurt.

"A text or a phone call I could probably get past. But he showed up here," Rawley said. He extended an arm over Case's shoulder to point at the hotel. "You mean something to him."

"Yeah, sure I do. A quick fuck and a payday, that's what I mean to him. That's all I've ever meant to any of them. I'm not worth anything beyond my tight ass and fat wallet. That's all anyone sees when they look at me—" Case stopped speaking when rage sparked in Rawley's deep-brown eyes, hands fisted at his sides. The sheriff was seriously pissed off, but Case had never felt safer, somehow knowing that neither the anger nor the fists would ever be directed at him.

"Get in the truck," Rawley bit out.

Case ran around the back of the truck to climb into the passenger seat before Rawley could change his mind. He really had no idea what he'd said that had made Rawley so angry, but he wasn't going to push the subject just yet. Case fastened his seat belt as Rawley reversed out of the lot onto the road. Rawley pointed the truck toward the edge of town and stomped on the accelerator. They drove for a good twenty minutes into the surrounding countryside, farmland on one side and forest on the other, until Rawley turned off the highway onto a dirt road grooved with roots. Weeds had long ago taken over the narrow drive that led into the nearby trees.

A short distance into the forest was a broken wood barricade with a Closed sign hanging off it at an angle. Rawley slowed the truck as he eased it around the blockade to continue down the dirt road on the other side. Case wasn't sure he'd be able to tell anyone where Rawley had taken him if asked because one dirt road looked like any other to him. The scenery outside the vehicle was amazing, but nothing compared to the beauty of the mercurial man sitting beside him. Rawley pulled into a thick copse of trees, branches scraping all sides of the vehicle, and parked. Silence engulfed them for several minutes after Rawley shut the rumbling engine off.

"Get out," Rawley finally said, keeping his eyes forward and his hands on the steering wheel.

Uncertainty pricked at him, but Case did as Rawley instructed. Tree limbs pressed in on him as he pushed the door open to climb out and work his way to the back of the truck where there was a small clearing. He watched through the back windshield as Rawley picked up his radio, spoke to someone briefly, and then got out of the cab to join Case. He shouldered past him to lower the tailgate before he yanked Case into his arms where he kissed him deeply until they were both breathless. Case ran his fingers through Rawley's hair and sucked on Rawley's bottom lip after he broke the kiss. Case never wanted to stop kissing the man.

Rawley groaned loudly as he spun Case to face the truck and bent him over the tailgate with a hand to the middle of his back. Rawley rocked his hips forward, pressing his groin against Case's ass as he reached around Case's hips. He worked the jeans open, pushed them down to Case's knees, and then lowered the zipper of his uniform pants. Case smiled at the soft hissing sound and bit his lip, still bent at the waist with his face pressed to warm metal. He wiggled his ass in invitation only to be rewarded with an open-palmed swat to the butt cheek that made his cock twitch in pleasure. He knew Rawley was going to fuck him; he wanted it, needed to feel the connection as Rawley moved inside him.

"Rawley," Case gasped as lubed fingers pushed past the tight ring of muscle of his pucker.

The thrusts were hard and fast but delivered with tightly controlled care; Rawley wasn't trying to hurt him. When Case began pushing back, trying to take the digits deeper in a silent plea for more, Rawley pulled his fingers free. Cool air caressed Case's overheated skin as Rawley moved away. He moaned in protest even as the unmistakable sound of a condom wrapper being torn open reached his ears. A heartbeat later, cold lubricated latex was placed against his pucker. Rawley wrapped strong fingers around his hips and pulled Case back as he pushed his own hips forward, plunging his entire length into Case's body. His breath caught as pain lanced through him at the sudden intrusion.

Rawley kissed the back of his neck before whispering, "I'm sorry. I thought you were ready."

"Me, too," Case grunted as he adjusted to Rawley's size, the pain easing to a slight burn from his entrance.

Once he relaxed sufficiently, he began to rock himself back and forth on the stiff shaft impaling him. Rawley took over with a steady, hammering pace that produced a stretching burn that kept him on the razor's edge of pain and pleasure. Case wanted more. The unrelenting tailgate dug into his thighs, bruising him with every thrust of Rawley's hips, though the truck seemed to be rocking beneath him. Rawley took Case's cock into his hand, stroking in time with his thrusts. The squeeze-release stroke punctuated by the occasional thumb across the slit was almost too much to take.

Case scraped his nails over the metal of the truck bed, eyes squeezed shut as he was carried away by the pleasure of Rawley's cock moving inside him. The knowledge that Rawley was fucking him in the middle of a forest, still dressed in his uniform, was all it took for Case to explode in Rawley's hand. Even as the final shudders of orgasm pulsed through his body, Rawley pulled out and turned him so they were facing each other. Strong hands circled his waist and Case found himself in awe as Rawley lifted him effortlessly onto the tailgate. He took Case's mouth in a heated kiss that Case responded to with fevered desperation. He'd just come, but he missed Rawley's fullness already. He was crazed with want.

Both men moved together awkwardly in their rushed attempt to free one of Case's legs from his jeans. One of his shoes fell to the ground, finally allowing an ankle to slip from the pants leg. Rawley turned his attention to his own pants, opening the belt and button to let them fall to the ground with a dull thud before he hooked Case's thighs and pulled him to the edge of the truck bed. After repositioning his cock against Case's tight pucker, he pushed back in with urgent thrusts. Feeling that fullness, that completion that he only got when Rawley was buried inside him, Case lay back into the bed of the truck with a satisfied moan. Lifting his legs, he rested his ankles on Rawley's shoulders as he gripped the edge of the tailgate to hold himself steady for Rawley's pounding thrusts, taking him as deeply as he could.

Case's focus narrowed in on Rawley. That handsome, rugged face was all he could see. Their grunts of exertion, moans of pleasure, and the sharp slap of flesh against flesh was all he could hear. The incredible burning stretch of Rawley's possession all he could feel. Every thought fled from his mind, every worry, every fear, until all he could think about was the intense pleasure only this man could give. Case knew in that moment he would do anything to keep this man in his life. Gasping for breath, he lifted his head to watch Rawley's face as he snapped his hips one last time, buried himself deeply inside Case, and came.

Rawley carefully lowered Case's legs as he pushed himself up from the truck bed. He was immediately engulfed in Rawley's hot embrace, his neck sucked and nibbled as Rawley shivered against him in postorgasmic bliss. Prickly stubble moved across his ear, along his jaw, as Rawley's lips made the trip back to Case's mouth. Case sucked on Rawley's tongue when it was thrust between his lips. He hugged Rawley tightly to his chest, hooking his ankles behind Rawley's thighs. His hole clenched around Rawley's softening dick and a shard of discomfort reminded him of the rough ride he'd just received. Rawley fisted his hair to pull his head back, forcing his lips apart.

"Never should have taken you home," Rawley whispered against his lips. "Should have called in and kept you with me." Rawley flexed his fingers to rub the base of Case's skull. Case slid a hand down Rawley's back to his ass where he cupped a firm, round butt cheek.

"You're more than a quick lay or a fat wallet, Casey," Rawley said, those intense brown eyes holding Case's gaze unwaveringly. "You are beauty, and warmth, and sunlight. If no one else can see that, then it's their loss."

Rawley eased his hips back, pulling free of Case's body. Case winced. After their impassioned coupling last night and the urgent, almost desperate fuck of the past few minutes, Case's ass was tender. In a few hours, he might find it difficult to sit properly, but for now, he was in a happy, sated place. Rawley quickly removed the condom and discarded it somewhere in the bed of the truck behind Case. Case's gaze leisurely moved over the gorgeous older man, taking in the tousled hair, rumpled shirt, the bare, muscular legs. The weight of the utility belt had pulled Rawley's pants down where they sat bunched around his ankles. Rawley's shirt hung down far enough to obscure his cock from view, but the sight of him disheveled and freshly fucked made Case's mouth water. The man was hands-down the most beautiful thing Case had ever seen.

"Damn, Sheriff Kane, you are one hot motherfucker," Case said.

Rawley blushed as he pulled his pants up and tucked his shirt in before running his fingers through his hair. Case smiled as he swung his legs contentedly on the tailgate, naked from the waist down except for his socks, and watched his man compose himself. His jeans were on the ground beneath him. He saw one of his shoes sitting on its side under a tree about five feet away. He had no idea where the other one had landed, and at the moment, he couldn't care less.

"I can't believe I just did that," Rawley muttered to himself, staring off into the distance behind Case. He cast a glance at Case, his gaze doing a quick sweep of his body before once again looking away. "Did I hurt you?"

"No. I'm sore, of course, but you can do that again anytime. You were amazing." Case continued to smile, swinging his sock-covered feet until Rawley shook his head and huffed out a small laugh. He picked up Case's jeans from the ground, brushed the dirt off as best he could, and then handed them to Case.

"Can you put your pants back on? We need to talk and I can't do that with you naked. You're too much of a distraction."

Case took the jeans as he jumped off the tailgate. Rawley hopped onto the back of the truck as Case fastened his jeans and retrieved the sneaker from beneath the tree, idly flipping it around in the air by the shoelace while he searched for its mate among the surrounding foliage. He found it a few feet away near the back tire of the truck. After shoving his feet back into the shoes, he rejoined Rawley in the truck bed, where the other man sat watching him, leaning back on his hands. They smiled at each other as their thighs and shoulders brushed together, warmth and a general sense of well-being suffusing every cell of Case's body. Rawley laced their fingers together in Case's lap as they took in the serene forest around them. They sat in silence for several minutes, enjoying the peace of the wilderness and the comfort of each other's company. When Rawley broke the silence, he did so with a soft voice.

"Leave him, Casey. Leave all of them. I can't be one among many."

Case glanced at Rawley from the corner of his eye and squeezed his hand. "I already did, weeks ago. Those men aren't what I want. I doubt they really ever were. The young, pretty type doesn't appeal to me anymore. I'm finding the older, mature, rough-around-the-edges type to be more my thing."

Rawley had some baggage he needed to work through, but Case knew he wanted to be the one to help him. Some men might look at Rawley and see a man who couldn't let go or move on. Case saw a man who loved with everything he had and would be fiercely loyal to whomever he gave his heart. Case wanted to be the man Rawley loved. When Rawley remained silent, Case stared into the distance and listened to a couple of birds chatter as recent events replayed in his head. His ass clenched at the memory of Rawley's rough entry, but one particular detail leaped to the front of his mind in sharp clarity. He folded a leg between them on the tailgate so that he was facing Rawley.

"Last night... I thought you said you hadn't had sex in two years. Did I misunderstand?" Case asked. He continued to hold Rawley's hand in one of his while lightly brushing the fine hairs of Rawley's forearm with the other. Their gazes locked when Rawley turned to look at him.

"No."

Unable to look into Rawley's eyes when he answered the next question, Case averted his gaze to Rawley's feet, swinging in and out of view. "So why did you have condoms and lube in your truck?"

Rawley cupped Case's chin. He then slid his palm along Case's jaw to grip the back of his neck, where he squeezed gently. Rawley pressed their foreheads together "I didn't," he answered. "I had them in my pocket. I put them there this morning before I took you home. I was... I had plans." Rawley shrugged.

"Oh." Case sighed, happy to know Rawley hadn't wanted to end their time together, either.

Rawley kissed him on the tip of the nose before pulling away. "I'm a mess. One minute, I tell myself to walk away before I get hurt; the next, I stuff a condom in my pocket. I don't want to have anything to do with a man who has six boyfriends, but when I'm with you, I forget all that and contemplate cuffing you to the bed so you can never leave. I've been one massive knot of contradictions since the moment I met you, Casey, and I don't like it."

"Why?" Case asked.

"I don't feel ready for another relationship." Rawley dropped his hand from Case's neck and looked down at their clasped hands. "Casey," Rawley said as Case shifted away so he could jump down from the truck bed.

Rawley tightened his hold on Case's hand, forcing him to pull and twist to get free. He walked a few feet away, hands on his hips, staring at the ground while trying to make sense of Rawley's words. His own emotions were a mess, which didn't help the situation. Rawley was definitely a guy who said one thing and did another, at least with him. Case had thought once they'd admitted their attraction, once they'd had sex, the mixed signals Rawley broadcasted would stop. Apparently, that was an incorrect assumption. If anything, it was all becoming more confusing than before.

"Casey—" Rawley started, but Case interrupted him.

"We haven't even been together twelve hours yet. Christ, we're still technically in the morning-after stage at this point. This could still turn out to be a one-night stand, and you're freaking out about a relationship?"

"You're the first man in two years who's even made me look twice. The only one since Alex died," Rawley said.

Case turned to face Rawley when he heard the irritated response, but he wasn't about to back down. He was irritated, too. "We've only had sex twice. Shit, I didn't even know you were gay until last night when you accosted me."

"I did not *accost* you." Rawley's voice rose in volume, which served to escalate Case right along with him.

"You're jumping so far ahead. Why does it have to be all or nothing with you? We can date and enjoy each other's company, even warm each other's beds without being in a relationship, you know. I may have been fucking six men, but I knew I wasn't in love with any of them. Sex and love *can* be independent of each other."

His own words rang true deep inside him. It made his heart ache and his stomach turn to actually put into words that there had been no love between him and the six men he'd shared several years of his life with. He finally understood that was why it had been so easy to walk away. Maybe he'd always known, but admitting he had been that shallow stung.

"Good for you," Rawley shouted as he pushed off the tailgate to stomp across the small clearing at the back of the truck. "You can screw without emotion. Congratulations. Proves my point that I'm just another convenient fuck for you, but whatever. I'm not wired that way, Casey. We wouldn't be here right now if you didn't mean something to me."

"You are not a convenient fuck, and you mean something to me, too, but we don't have to be in a relationship yet. Can't we just date for a while before you make a committed couple out of us? I don't understand why you can't just enjoy being with me."

"Because it makes me feel guilty. Every time you make me smile or laugh, or just happy, I feel guilty, but maybe I wouldn't if it was...more."

The fight in Case was crushed immediately by Rawley's tortured tone. The idea that starting a new relationship would cure the pain of losing someone deeply loved, or that a new love would obliterate the lost one seemed ridiculous to Case, but this intelligent man truly believed what he was saying. There wasn't a single word Case could think of that would help, so he remained silent, watching the man he cared about waging an internal war he couldn't understand.

Rawley threaded his fingers through his hair as he paced in a tight circle. Case wanted so much to offer his man comfort, but he didn't really know how to go about it. One of his past boyfriends, Richard, had had an anxiety disorder. He had told Case that during panic attacks, he needed help getting out of his head. While grief and guilt weren't the same as panic, maybe the same rule applied. Maybe pulling Rawley out of his head would help.

"Why would you feel guilty about being happy?" Case asked. He could feel Rawley's anguish as if it were his own. Rawley stopped pacing and dropped his hands, facing away from Case.

"Get in the truck. I'll take you home," Rawley said softly. It wasn't the answer Case wanted. He approached the truck but stopped behind Rawley, fighting the intense desire to take the man in his arms. He stood as close as he dared and kept his voice soft, calm.

"Please, Rawley. Tell me why you think Alex would want you to be miserable. If he loved you even half as much as you love him, he would want you to be happy, wouldn't he? To move on and live your life."

"It's not about Alex," Rawley said. "It's about me. You don't...know."

"Then tell me."

Rawley continued to stare off into the distance. He remained silent so long Case thought he would never answer.

"It's my fault he's dead. I killed him by being too stubborn and too cocky. We worked together in the Denver PD. We were in separate vehicles, but more often than not we found ourselves at the same crime scenes. One night, we both responded to a domestic disturbance call. You never know which way those things will go. He told me..." Rawley shook his head. "He told me we needed backup, but I said we could handle it. Shit hit the fan right away. It all happened so fast, but we both got shot. I was shot twice—one in my shoulder and one in my hip. Alex only got shot once, but he took it in the chest. I don't even know exactly when he died... All I know is that I'm alive and he isn't."

A bird chirped from a nearby tree, breaking the heavy silence with its happy song. It was surreal that Rawley would share such a tragic, traumatizing event while birds sang in the trees and the sun filtered through the leaves so beautifully. He was overcome with such an intense need to comfort Rawley, but Case was fairly certain he was reliving the shooting in his mind, and he wasn't certain how touch would be received.

"Rawley." Case said his name, hoping to bring him back to the present gently. Startling a cop with PTSD just didn't seem like a smart idea, so he waited a moment before trying again. "Rawley, can I touch you?"

"Why would you want to?" Rawley softly asked.

Now that Rawley was safely out of his head and aware of Case's presence, Case closed the short distance between their bodies to press against Rawley's back. He put his hands on Rawley's sides, just above his utility belt. He gauged Rawley's reaction, which was nothing, before wrapping his arms around Rawley's waist and holding him. It was painful for Case to learn that this man, someone he admired and was quickly coming to care for, would believe something so irrational. There was no guarantee that even if they had followed procedure to the letter, done everything right, Alex would have walked away from that call alive. No one could see into the future or stop a bullet. Nothing Case said would change the beliefs Rawley held or change the past, erase the memories or the pain, but he could hold him. He could be there for him and maybe one day prove that Rawley deserved every ounce of his love.

Chapter Seventeen

TWO DAYS HAD passed since Case last saw or spoke to Rawley, and he was beginning to feel itchy. They had crossed each other's paths or seen the other in passing almost every day since Rawley picked him up from the side of the road, so his man's absence was noticeable. Case did see Jordan on a daily basis, however, and that only heightened his awareness that Rawley wasn't around. Jordan couldn't seem to get it through his head that Case was no longer interested. The infuriating man kept showing up at Aunt Sylvia's front door. Hostess that she was, she always invited him in, asked him to stay for lunch or dinner, or suggested a hike around the property.

Case didn't know what she was doing, considering she knew their history, but every morning, she would tell him there was no reason to be rude. Case scoffed at that. He could be mean, rude, and downright insulting—Jordan would still cling. Case's bank account pretty much ensured the continued attention. His past actions didn't help the situation. He'd frequently been hateful to the men in his life, only to turn around and give them exactly what they wanted—a hard fuck and a check. Jordan had no reason to expect anything different.

But things were very different for Case. He had left that life behind him and he didn't miss it. The slower, easygoing nature of Clover City and its inhabitants was growing on him. The fact the town was more appealing to him now that he was falling head over heels for the sheriff was not lost on him. Unfortunately, the object of his affection had gone MIA. On the way home from the grocery store the day before, Case had stopped by the police station only to be told that Rawley had taken the week off. Hopeful they had a full six days to get to know each other, Case had driven to Rawley's house to find the truck gone. It had been the same thing today.

Case was regretting his own words about them not being in a committed relationship because Rawley had apparently taken them to heart. He'd taken time off, left without a word, and Case had no way of contacting him. It once again occurred to Case that he needed to get Rawley's phone number, but he kept forgetting to ask given the usual ease of finding the man. Confused and a little hurt, Case drove to the McKesson Farm in search of friendly ears and like minds.

Jake was driving out of the barn on the biggest tractor that Case had ever seen, and he waved as Case turned into the driveway. He saw Ryan on the far side of the barn chopping wood as he parked the car and got out. He inhaled the clean, fresh air, turning his face up toward the sun for a moment before heading to the barn. Case had no idea what he really wanted out of this visit, but these men were the only ones he'd become friends with in this town. They'd connected at the barbecue and Jake had called Aunt Sylvia's every night just to talk. Shutting the tractor off, Jake jumped down when Case approached him.

"Hi," Case said in greeting.

"Hey there. So, what brings a rich city boy like you to a boring farm like mine?"

"Same thing that brought Ryan, I guess. Attraction. Desire. Maybe love." Case exhaled loudly.

"Oh, sweetheart, I'm sorry, but I'm already taken," Jake said with exaggerated sadness.

"Damn right, you're taken," Ryan grumbled as he came around the barn to join them.

Case smiled and fluttered his eyelashes. "Come on, Jake. Run away with me. I have money."

Jake laughed as Ryan grabbed Case in a brotherly choke hold, rubbing his knuckles painfully into Case's skull.

"You're damn lucky I know you're kidding."

After Ryan released him, Case massaged his abused scalp while fingering his hair back into place. Ryan rested his arm over Case's shoulders and the unexpected friendly affection was his undoing. He buried his face in Ryan's shoulder, hugged him around the waist, and let the tears fall. Jake pressed against his back and the couple held him until he managed to get himself under control. Case straightened, embarrassed about breaking down in front of them, and wiped the tears from his face.

"Sorry," he mumbled.

"It's not a problem," Ryan said.

"Anytime you need us, we're right here," Jake added.

Case huffed out a breath. Jake was still holding him around the waist with his chin resting on Case's shoulder when he asked, "Want to come inside and talk?"

"Yeah."

Once Jake released him, Case followed the man back to the house. Ryan motioned for Case to follow him to the back porch where he directed Case to the patio set arranged around a fire-pit while Jake branched off to go inside. Ryan chose one of the cushioned patio chairs closest to the pit and propped his feet up on the short stone wall surrounding it. Case chose one of the lounge chairs, kicked his shoes off, and tucked his feet beneath him. Jake returned with beers, handing them each one before claiming the chair nearest Ryan and linking their fingers. The unapologetic show of affection caused Case's heart to ache, so he looked away for a few seconds as he took a swallow of ice-cold brew.

"Okay, start talking. Is this about Mr. Corvette?" Jake asked, and Case jerked his gaze back to the men.

"Small town," Ryan reminded him. "Everyone knows he's here and why. I ran into him at the gas station. He's not shy about telling people he's your boyfriend."

Case looked at his beer and grunted in annoyance. Damn that man. If Jordan was claiming they were together to everyone he met, it might explain Rawley's disappearing act. Case mentally added anger to his list of mixed emotions. He'd known leaving his old life behind wouldn't be easy, but he'd expected the struggle to be internal. He hadn't expected the guys to put up such a fight. Jordan was ruining his opportunity with Rawley, and it was pissing him off. What would it take to get through Jordan's head—all of their heads—that it was over? Case placed his beer down on the wrought-iron table beside him and rubbed his temples to ease the headache forming behind his eyes.

"I don't know what to do." Case looked at Ryan and then at Jake. "Jordan is not my boyfriend. He never was. He was just a guy I slept with on occasion. I can't seem to get it through his head that I'm not interested in going there again."

"I'm...confused. I thought you said you were in love," Jake said.

"Maybe. Maybe in love, but not with Jordan. With Rawley."

Jake and Ryan glanced at each other. Ryan lifted his eyebrows at Jake and shrugged as a devilish smile spread across Jake's face that made Case nervous when it was directed at him.

"Start at the beginning and tell me *everything*," Jake said.

Case shook his head as he returned the smile. Jake was apparently going to be his gossipy tell-all friend while Ryan would be the strong cry-on-my-shoulder friend. He would be sure to thank his aunt for suggesting he visit Clover City and for introducing him to these two. There was no doubt in his mind that he would always be able to count on them being in his corner. They were the first true friends Case had ever had. Ryan sat silently, not reacting much as Case recounted his short twelve-hour stint with Rawley punctuated by Jordan's unexpected arrival. Jake on the other hand, reacted dramatically, instantly improving Case's mood with his antics and making him feel somewhat justified in his feelings.

"So, the sheriff just left?" Ryan asked, once Case finished talking.

"He never struck me as a coward," Jake added. "He's always faced things head-on before."

"Well, this is new territory for him," Case said in Rawley's defense. The man had hurt him by disappearing, but that didn't change how Case felt about him.

"It's new territory for you, too, from what you just told us," Ryan pointed out.

"Yes, it is," Case admitted before polishing off the remainder of his beer. Jake took the empty bottles and then went inside to get more.

"You came to Clover City to get your head on straight and change your life. You've said that more than once," Ryan said. "It seems to me that getting involved with a guy who's not emotionally available isn't the best thing. He took off on you, Case. Jordan, however, came all this way—"

"Not the same thing," Case interrupted. "Jordan wants my money, not me."

"Are you sure about that? Clover City is a long drive to make for just money," Ryan said as Jake came back outside, handing them both fresh beers.

Case stared at Ryan for a moment while the suggestion sank in. The truth was, he didn't know what Jordan or any of the others actually felt because he'd never asked. When Jordan showed up, Case had assumed he wanted sex and money. He deflated completely, lying back on the lounge to stare up at the cloudless blue sky.

"I am such an ass. A shallow, egotistical ass." Case sat back up to face his friends.

"Don't like that idea, huh? That Jordan might love you?" Ryan asked, looking a little smug.

"I still don't think he loves me, not really, but him showing up makes a little more sense if *he* thinks he does. I mean, if I knew where Rawley was, you can damn sure bet I'd chase his ass down." Both men smiled at him knowingly. "It's not the same thing, though. There are things about Rawley you don't know that make him disappearing like this...a different thing than me just leaving town."

"Okay." Jake nodded, but Case had the feeling he was just placating him.

If Case had thought talking to Jake and Ryan would help him clarify things, he'd been delusional. All it did was make him more confused, because now he had Jordan's feelings added to the mix. Case shook his head before finishing off his beer. He needed to actually have a conversation with Jordan to flush out the true reason behind his prolonged visit.

"I'm going to head out. Things to do. Thank you for the beer and listening." Case stretched after sitting for so long. Plus, all his emotional baggage and stress were making his muscles tense.

"Are you okay to drive?" Jake asked as both men stood as well.

"Yeah, I'm good. I used to be a heavy partier. It takes more than two beers to give me a buzz," Case answered with a smile. "Thanks for asking, though. No one's ever cared before."

"Then you've had some shitty friends," Jake said.

"Don't I know it," Case mumbled.

The couple stayed with him all the way around the house to his car where they exchanged hugs and promises to get together again soon. Case left McKesson Farm determined to fix the mess he found himself in. He couldn't do anything about Rawley until the man returned, but he could deal with Jordan right then.

IT WAS JUST after noon, so Jordan was probably just getting out of bed. Hopefully, by catching Jordan half asleep with his guard down, Case would get an honest answer from him about his little two-week visit. Even if he found out Jordan was in love with him, he wouldn't be getting involved with him again, but at least he'd have a better idea of how to handle the situation. There had to have been something beyond Jordan's looks that had attracted Case in the first place. Maybe Case could find that something again and they could be friends.

Case drove to the Cloverleaf Hotel, noting the absence of Rawley's truck in front of the police station as he passed and parked in the spot next to Jordan's Corvette. Case sighed heavily as the small hope that Rawley was back at work died. He got out of the car and went inside the hotel where the same cute, young man as before stood behind the desk working. The young man looked up and smiled when Case approached the desk and rested his elbows on top. Jordan was staying there on Case's dime, but Case hadn't asked what room he'd be in. He'd never planned on seeing Jordan in his room.

"Welcome to the Cloverleaf Hotel. My name is Trent. How can I help you?"

"I'm here to see Jordan Caskill, but I don't know what room he's in," Case answered.

Trent picked up the phone. "Who should I say is here?"

"Case."

Trent's gaze snapped to Case's face as his entire body stiffened, the blush Case remembered from his first visit spreading across Trent's cheeks. Jordan's outgoing, flirtatious personality must have worked its magic with Trent. Case looked the younger man over. Trent was about the same age as Jordan, had short blond hair and soft brown eyes. The slight redness of his cheeks was an attractive addition to the cream-toned skin. A couple of weeks ago, Case might have slept with the cutie. He was exactly the type of guy Case had been interested in before Rawley drove into his life. Trent was most definitely the type Jordan had been known to hook up with, which made his obsession with Case that much stranger.

"I'm not his boyfriend, and as far as I know, he's free," Case said to Trent. He didn't know if Jordan and Trent had already hooked up or not, but he hoped the information would alleviate some of Trent's discomfort. Case straightened as Trent's gaze slid over his body. The action was timid, but it was suddenly obvious it wasn't Jordan that Trent had set his sights on. Case would be careful this time, take the younger man's feelings into consideration, and let him down as easily as possible. Case was flattered, but he didn't need to fight off an additional man's attentions while trying to entice Rawley into dating.

Trent's cheeks became a deeper shade of red as he spoke into the phone. "Case is here asking to see you." Jordan had most definitely been working his magic if Trent's relaxed, familiar tone and embarrassment was anything to go by. Without another word to Jordan, he hung up the phone. He spoke to Case but didn't look at him.

"Hold on one minute," he said before disappearing through a door in the wall behind him. An older woman followed Trent out of the room and took up the station behind the desk while Trent waved Case to follow him. "This way." Case followed him to the elevator, confused. He could have found his own way to the room if Trent had given him the number.

"So, what's going on?" Case asked once they were alone inside the elevator.

"Jordan asked me to show you to his room," Trent answered quietly, shifting on his feet nervously.

Case nodded and stared at the closed doors. He considered asking Trent why Jordan wanted him to show Case the way, but he had a feeling he already knew. If Jordan was staying true to form, he was hoping Case's past predilection for as much dick at once as possible would result in a threesome. Case wondered if the constant crimson of Trent's face meant he knew what Jordan was planning.

He hated that Jordan was playing with this guy's desires the way he was, and he tried to remember if he'd ever been guilty of the same thing. Nothing immediately came to mind, but it bothered him to consider it all the same. The elevator stopped on the second floor, and Case followed Trent down the hall to room 212. A moment after Trent knocked on the door, Jordan answered, wearing boxers that were impressively tented in the front. Case sighed and looked away in annoyance as his suspicions regarding Jordan's motives were proven correct.

Jordan whistled. "I could open my door to the two of you all day every day."

Trent turned a darker shade of red, if that was possible, as he glanced quickly at Case. Case bit down his irritation and kept his face a blank mask. He wasn't going to do anything to encourage Jordan or anything that would upset Trent since he was already clearly uncomfortable. Jordan, completely oblivious to the heightened emotions swirling in the hallway, took Trent's hand to pull him into his arms while backing into the room.

"How much time do you have?" Jordan purred, palming Trent's butt.

"An hour. I took my lunch break," Trent answered and wrapped his arms around Jordan's neck.

This was definitely not the first time Jordan had taken Trent in his arms, or to his bed. No wonder Trent had been uncomfortable from the moment Case had announced himself; the poor guy thought Jordan was cheating every time they were together. Case bit his tongue so he wouldn't mention how casually Jordan was handling Trent. It was all a game to him. Case hated that, up until a week ago, he would have done the same thing and not thought twice about who he was hurting. He remained in the hall, watching the two through the doorway. Jordan grabbed the hem of Trent's shirt and pulled it over his head. He spun Trent around so he could see Case through the door while his pants were opened. Jordan held Trent against his chest as he slid a hand over Trent's abs and down into his underwear where he fondled him.

"Come here, lover. You know you want a piece of this." Jordan stared directly into Case's eyes as he licked a path up Trent's neck to the lobe of his ear, where he bit down. Trent's eyes closed with a quavering sigh as he carded his fingers through Jordan's hair. "He's got a tight ass, a big cock, and the most delicious spunk."

Case dropped his chin to his chest, shook his head, and sighed. Dirty talk like that used to be all it would take to get him hard. Not only had his interest in Jordan evaporated, so had his reaction to Jordan's words. He wouldn't mind hearing a few obscene words and suggestions from Rawley, though. He smiled at the thought of the sheriff whispering dirty nothings into his ear, and the meaning behind the smile was immediately misunderstood by Jordan.

"Yeah, baby, I knew you'd want him." Jordan released Trent long enough to remove his boxers. Once free of the tight cloth, he palmed his erect dick and licked his lips. "Come fuck us, lover."

Jordan lay on the bed, spreading his legs in invitation as he continued to lazily stroke himself. Trent walked up to timidly kiss Case on the neck, just above his collar. Case hugged him tightly, gave him a chaste peck on the temple, and whispered into his ear.

"I'm sorry, but this isn't going to happen." Case ran a hand over Trent's hair as the man sagged against him, hiding his face in Case's neck. Case glared at Jordan for putting Trent up to this. As shy as he was, he was probably horribly humiliated by the situation. Trent pulled away and turned his back, refusing to meet Case's eyes while he refastened his pants. Case gently grabbed him by the shoulders and turned him around, forcing Trent to look at him.

"My heart belongs to someone else. We won't be lovers, but we can be friends. I'd like to have a few friends when I move here," Case said with a smile.

After a moment, Trent smiled back. Completely ignoring Jordan, Case walked back down the hallway to the bank of elevators. The room door clicked shut behind him, and he glanced back to see if he was still alone. Case was a mess of emotions as he rode back down to the first floor and left the hotel on autopilot. He'd started this day thinking he would finalize a few things, get all of his affairs figured out and settled, but all he'd managed to do was make things worse for himself. At least, that's how he was feeling as he walked across the lot to the Mustang.

Once again, his gaze darted over to the police station where the parking space reserved for the sheriff remained empty. As screwed up as everything still was, Case at least knew where he stood with Jordan. He didn't have a clue where he stood with Rawley, though he was beginning to get a very painful idea if he judged solely by the disappearing act. Rawley wasn't ready, and he didn't want anything more involved than a roll in the hay. It hurt that he'd taken off for a week without a word, especially at such a sensitive time. Plenty of men had rejected Case after getting what they wanted, and he'd always managed to move on. Maybe he'd explore things with Trent someday, maybe not. At the moment, he wanted to go home and let himself fall to pieces, wallow in self-pity over how empty his life was turning out to be, and pine for a man he couldn't have.

Chapter Eighteen

IMMEDIATELY AFTER DROPPING Case at home following their unexpected session in the woods, Rawley had returned to the station. He told his deputies he was taking a week off, officially handed the reins over to Ted, and drove to Denver, arriving shortly after sunset that same day. He'd needed time away from Case to think about everything that had happened and evaluate his feelings. Plus, he had a few demons he needed to exorcise.

The first stop he'd made the following Monday morning was the house where he and Alex had been shot. Rawley stayed in the truck, idling on the curb, just staring blankly at the cottage-style home. He didn't see the red front door that in his memory was a peeling dark blue. Or the lawn that had green grass now instead of the dirt he had bled onto. He was lost to the memory of that night—the spark of the muzzle blast, the echo of gunshots, and the smell of blood as he fought to stay conscious. Oddly, he didn't remember any physical pain, only a cold numbness spreading through his limbs.

When Rawley emerged from the memory, he was crying. Even in the flashback, he wasn't aware of Alex being shot. He still didn't know exactly when the man he'd loved had left this world, and that was an emotional scar he would bear deep in his soul forever. He took a few moments to compose himself before putting the truck back in gear and driving to his old precinct.

Rawley parked the truck at the back of the lot where those on duty left their personal vehicles while on shift. He still recognized many of the cars as belonging to cops he'd been closely acquainted with—the men he had worked long, hard hours with for years. To the left was a locked gate that led into the back lot of the precinct where the squad cars were kept. A short distance down the block was the impound where Rawley could see a guard sitting in the booth, flipping through a magazine.

The dashboard clock told him it was still fifteen minutes before shift change so he killed the engine and got out. He lowered the tailgate to sit on, ready to wait for his ex-colleagues to call it a day. While he sat, the familiar routines of the police station he'd once referred to as his second home going on around him, his mind wandered to Case and the last time the tailgate had been lowered. It had only been a little over twenty-four hours since he'd seen the man, but he already missed him; that beautiful face with those smoky-blue eyes that never failed to brighten Rawley's day. He was swinging his feet and smiling when a deep voice boomed across the lot from the gate.

"Sargent Rawley Kane, you old son of a bitch. Is that really you?"

The voice belonged to Devon Kruze, a hulking mass of bald flab who frequently rubbed people the wrong way. When Rawley had still been on the force, Kruze had been partnered with a younger female officer who was constantly complaining about his inappropriateness, not only with her, but with every woman he came into contact with. The misogynistic behavior was probably the reason behind him continually being passed over for promotion. The captain was female.

"Yep, it's me."

Rawley hopped off the tailgate to greet Kruze and the three other officers with him—Trevor Dean, Scott Wymer, and Dan Carpenter. Along with Alex, the six of them had gotten wildly drunk on more than one occasion after a rough shift or a dangerous call. None of these men had known Rawley and Alex went home together after their gatherings. Rawley had planned on telling them tonight over drinks, but he was now rethinking that idea. He didn't feel the camaraderie he'd felt two years ago. They'd worked the streets together for nearly a decade, but he felt closer to his deputies and the townsfolk of Clover City than these cops.

"What brings you back here?" Wymer asked. "Last we heard you'd taken off to parts unknown."

Rawley shrugged. "Got someone new in my life and realized I was still holding onto old memories, so I came back to close that chapter."

"Someone new? I never saw you with a girl all the years we worked together. I was starting to think you were a fairy," Carpenter said.

Wymer punched him in the arm, laughing, as Kruze clapped Rawley on the shoulder. "Nah, Kane's no queer. You wouldn't believe what this place is turning into, Kane. Damn chicks running the place and now they're letting dykes and fags in."

"Careful, dude. Anyone can hear you out here, and you know the captain will force you to sit through that stupid diversity class if she finds out," Dean said.

Rawley was enraged. It took everything he had not to slap Kruze's hand off his shoulder and knock his fat ass to the ground. Maybe because he and Alex had never been "out" as a gay couple, or they'd deliberately turned a deaf ear, he'd never realized how hatefully bigoted these men were. Rawley had encountered homophobia plenty of times before, but he no longer had a tolerance for it.

"Maybe attending a diversity class would be a good thing for all of you," Rawley said, turning to lift the tailgate closed. He was going to keep this little reunion extremely short. He reached into his pocket to pull out his keys as he faced his ex-coworkers again. "Just stopped by to say hi, but I'll be on my way now."

"Hey, Kane, we're heading to the Brew House for a drink if you want to join us," Wymer said as Rawley walked around the truck and opened the door.

He climbed behind the wheel and started the engine before looking over his shoulder at men he'd once considered friends. "No, thanks. Got a man waiting for me back home."

With those words hanging in the air, Rawley closed his door, put the truck in gear, and drove away, laughing at the shocked faces he'd left in his dust. He smiled the entire drive back to his hotel where he ordered dinner from the room-service menu. He felt a million pounds lighter. The location of the shooting wasn't as dark, ugly, and horrible as his memories cast it, whereas his old colleagues were worse than he remembered. It was the reality check he'd hoped it would be, and he was almost done cutting ties to his past.

The following morning, he called Dr. Rodgers, the psychiatrist he'd been assigned to after the shooting, to schedule an appointment for Thursday afternoon. Rawley really had no idea what he was going to do all day Tuesday or Wednesday, and found that not having a plan allowed his mind to wander. He spent the entire day Tuesday watching movies in his room, thinking about Case, wondering which part of the city he'd lived in. Was it possible they'd crossed paths before? Rawley imagined a party boy with multiple boyfriends and more money than was good for him would have had a few run-ins with the law.

On more than one occasion, he picked up his phone, only to remember he didn't have Case's cell number. He considered dialing Sylvia's house number but ended up just dropping the phone on the bed and returning his attention to whatever he was watching. Rawley didn't know what he would say if Case did pick up the line.

Hi, beautiful. I miss you. I wish I'd brought you with me. That would work, but he wasn't ready...yet.

Rawley wanted Case by his side, but not in Denver where five of Case's six ex-lovers were residing. He had a difficult enough time dealing with the one ex back in Clover City. Jealousy flared to life in his chest right alongside a healthy dose of fear. He'd left Case without a word, alone, with an ex-boyfriend determined to win him back. This trip had been necessary as far as Rawley was concerned, but his timing could have been better. His anxiety had him reaching for the phone again. The display told him it was after midnight, but Case was more than likely still awake. Despite that, Rawley dropped the cell, shut the television off, and rolled over, intent on getting some sleep.

Wednesday was spent visiting all the places Rawley and Alex liked to go together. Two years ago, all Rawley saw when he walked down the street was the theater where Alex had first kissed him, the restaurant where Alex had suggested they move in together, or the lake where they would sit, holding hands while feeding the geese. As Rawley strolled through the streets, diverting to take a leisurely walk in the park, he smiled. He had wonderful, loving memories of Alex and found he was eager to make new ones with Case. Except when he imagined sitting by a lake with Case, it was the one at the back of Sylvia's property. The movies would be at the quaint two-screen theater in downtown Clover City; the restaurant, Hannah's Bistro on Second Avenue.

As Wednesday rolled into Thursday, Rawley was becoming more restless. He wanted to get back to Clover City so he could spend the rest of his life wrapped around Casey Holden. His appointment with Dr. Rodgers was later in the day, so he had hours ahead of him with nothing to occupy his mind. After a long shower followed by a lazy breakfast in bed, he lowered the volume on the television and pulled up Facebook. He had an account, but it had been months since he'd logged on. Rawley signed in and searched for Casey Holden. The profile picture of his beautiful man gave him an instant smile and aching erection.

Rawley spent hours cyberstalking his boy, soaking in all the information he could about Case's life pre-Clover City. He was smiling in most of the pictures, but Rawley could tell it was forced. Those amazing smoke-blue eyes didn't reflect the happiness Rawley had rapidly grown accustomed to seeing. By the time his appointment with Dr. Rodgers occurred, he was feeling the happiest and most hopeful he had in years.

"Sergeant Kane." Dr. Rodgers smiled as he greeted Rawley with a firm handshake. "It's good to see you again. You look much better than the last time you were in here."

"Thank you. I'm doing better, a lot better."

"Come on in. Have a seat anywhere. Tell me what's new in your life."

Dr. Rodgers waited until Rawley sat in the overstuffed armchair before moving to the sofa to take a seat himself. The man's demeanor was open, warm, not at all like Rawley remembered, and he relaxed into the cushion.

"Well, first off, it's Sheriff Kane now, but you can drop the formality. Call me Rawley. I find the small-town familiarity suits me better."

"Wow! Congratulations. That's a huge step forward," Dr. Rodgers said, and Rawley smiled back at the man. "So, you left Denver and got your life back on track. That's excellent, but something brought you back to my door."

"I need closure," Rawley told him.

"Okay. Tell me how I can help with that."

"I need to know if the advice you gave me years ago would've changed if I'd been honest. If I'd told you that Alex and I were more than coworkers on the force. We were a committed couple. I loved him."

Once the words were out, Rawley released a slow breath, trying to stop the panic attack he felt coming on. Dr. Rodgers waited patiently while Rawley composed himself. When their gazes met again, the doctor smiled.

"That was hard for you."

Rawley had a lump in his throat, so he chose to nod his affirmation rather than attempt to speak.

"For what it's worth, I had already come to that conclusion...years ago." Dr. Rodgers smiled warmly when Rawley stared at him in surprise. "And no, my advice wouldn't have been different. What happened was awful. You were seriously injured. Someone you cared about was killed and laid to rest before you even knew he was gone. It doesn't matter that you were in the hospital undergoing surgery. What matters is that when you woke up, you were alone and your entire world was turned upside down."

Rawley averted his gaze to stare at the trees outside the window across the room, their leaves rustling in the gentle evening breeze. The sky was the same shade of gray-blue as Case's eyes and the next words were out of his mouth before he realized he'd spoken out loud.

"Casey put it right."

Dr. Rodgers smiled. "And who is Casey?"

"He's a guy I met after his car broke down. He made me realize how stagnant and lonely and boring my life had become."

Rawley spent the remainder of his allotted time telling Dr. Rodgers about Casey Holden and everything he found attractive about the young man. They discussed Rawley's thoughts and feelings about the man, as well as the situation they were facing as a couple. When the hour was up, Rawley was still uncertain about his future with Case, but at least he was more comfortable moving forward with a relationship. Dr. Rodgers walked with him to the door but stopped before opening it.

"Rawley, you said you came here for closure, but I think you know the closure you really want isn't here. It's in Fairmount Cemetery."

Rawley did know that. He'd never visited Alex's grave even though it had been Dr. Rodgers's suggestion from the beginning that he go, but eventually Rawley had left Denver without once seeing his partner's final resting place. They said their goodbyes and Rawley left with Dr. Rodgers's best wishes for his new relationship with Case. It had only been a one-hour session, but Rawley was exhausted. He had no trouble falling asleep that night immediately after finishing his dinner. The scotch he'd taken from the minibar would help keep the nightmares at bay so he could sleep soundly. He was heading home the next day, but he wouldn't leave Denver a second time without making that all-important stop.

Morning dawned with high winds blowing dark rain clouds in from the mountains. *A somber day for a somber moment*, Rawley thought as he parked the truck and went in search of the plot he wanted. Once he found it, he just stared at it, letting the tears fall. The grief felt different now, less consuming than it had before. Two years ago, he'd felt like his life was over if Alex wasn't in it, but at some point, without being aware of it, he'd started healing, moving on, and he was falling in love again.

Sitting in the grass, he leaned his shoulder against the large headstone. Rawley reached over to trace his fingers over the letters engraved into the granite—Alexander David Dassinger. He smiled when he remembered how many times he'd joked with Alex about his initials being ADD and how appropriate they were to his hyperactive personality. The man had always been so energetic and excitable. Apparently, that was a trait Rawley was attracted to since Case exhibited the same.

"I miss you," Rawley murmured. "I'd say I'm sorry I got you shot, but I know now I'm not to blame. Not really. It was the asshole who pulled the trigger. You know, I found him. A few weeks before I moved away, I found the fucker totally coked out in a strip club. I'd gone in with the mindset to kill him, but he was doing such a good job of it himself, I just walked away. Called in a tip to Carpenter and just...left town."

Rawley shook his head as he looked around the serene graveyard. A busy street lay directly on the other side of the northern fence, but where Alex was buried, the sounds of traffic were completely lost in the wind.

"I love you. A deep, special part of me reserved just for you always will, but I met someone. His name is Casey Holden, and I think of him as my own personal tsunami. When I saw him coming, I knew he was going to be life-changing and that nothing would be the same once he hit, but I couldn't do a damn thing to stop him. I just stood there and let him wash over me. We haven't spent a lot of time talking, so I haven't gotten much information out of him, just a lot of emotional turmoil and mind-blowing sex. But I've watched him, and he approaches life like it's one big party for him to enjoy. It's hard to be grumpy wearing a T-shirt with a unicorn farting a cloud of glitter.

"What I've gathered through my infamous snooping online is that he's quite a bit younger than me, maybe ten or twelve years. He's got thick dark hair and gorgeous smoky-blue eyes, smooth skin, a perfect body. You would have loved him; he's so damn beautiful and vibrant. He has so much love to give, and all he wants is to be loved back. I like to think I can do that. I know I can do that."

A strong gust of wind, smelling distinctly of rain, had Rawley glancing up at the darkening sky. The stormy weather approaching perfectly mirrored his current psychological state.

"You wouldn't recognize the person I am when he's around. I'm so damn possessive and jealous and sex-crazed. I've done things with him

I've never done before. He gave me a blow job in the front seat of the truck, and I fucked him over the tailgate in the middle of the woods while in uniform. The real kicker is I think I fell in love with him the moment I laid eyes on him. So many things kept me away from him at first. I kept telling myself he was too young; he was just visiting; he would never want me when he had six men here in Denver waiting for him, though he says they only want sex and money."

Rawley laughed. Dropping his chin to his chest, he smiled like an idiot. He was talking to a piece of stone like it was a person.

"I'm a dork, sitting here talking about a man I clearly don't know a lot about and claiming to love him. I can hear your voice in my head, Alex, asking me how that's possible. I can't explain it, maybe it isn't love. Maybe it's just a serious case of loneliness and a hot ass to cure it, but I don't think so. Anyway, I'm going after him. He's worth the fight; God knows there will be a fight. One I may already be losing. One of Casey's ex-boy toys showed up Sunday morning and made it very clear he wants Casey back. That's why I've got to go. I have to get back to him, but I wanted you to know I'm doing well and moving on, just like everyone has been telling me to do."

Rawley sat for several more minutes, watching the storm blow in as he reflected on everything that had happened. It was hard to believe it had only been two weeks since Casey had arrived—his outgoing personality and youthful vigor changing Rawley's life one sexy smile at a time. A drop of rain hit his head, so Rawley decided it was time to get on the road, especially if he wanted to make it back to Clover City before dark. He pushed to his feet and looked down at Alex's grave one last time.

"Love you," he murmured before walking back to his truck.

MOST OF THE drive home, Rawley was filled with relief that he'd finally left the guilt-laden sorrow behind him. Though he would always hold onto Alex and the love they'd shared, the memories they'd made, he felt more than ready to offer Case a relationship. But the closer he got to Clover City, the more anxious he became that Case wouldn't want what he offered. During their post-sex fight in the woods, Case had said he wasn't asking for a relationship, just a date, and afterward Rawley had left town without a word.

Rawley slowed the truck and pulled to the side of the road. After shutting off the engine, he sat there, listening to the wind blow through the long grass of a nearby field. It was warm outside, humid. The rainstorm he'd been driving through for the past several hours had finally blown farther east. He stared out the front windshield as he fought the strong desire to detour to Sylvia's cabin before returning to his own house. Six days without Case was getting to him.

Rawley thought he needed a hot shower and a change of clothes before approaching Case, but on a deeper level, he didn't want to be away from Case one minute longer. He was still afraid that he had been another notch on Case's bedpost, or that Case had returned to his ex during Rawley's absence. The thought that he'd lost Case before he ever had him made Rawley's chest hurt so he pushed that possibility aside, refusing to give it weight. Instead, he chose to believe that Case was either going out of his head with worry or was royally pissed. He couldn't wait to see which way his man had gone, though either way was a good sign. It meant Case really did care about him. Rawley had plans for Case, including dinner out followed by a night spent with Case tucked securely in his arms.

Deciding against going home first, despite feeling grungy, Rawley started the truck and headed for his man. The road was wet from recent rainfall, meaning Sylvia's driveway was little more than mud when he turned into it. A weight was lifted off Rawley's chest when bright gold greeted his eyes and he parked behind Case's Mustang. He wasn't sure how to feel about the other two vehicles parked along the side of the drive. The ex-boyfriend's black Corvette was a few feet in front of Jake's beat-up old Chevy truck.

It didn't sit well with him that Case's ex was still in town, but he wasn't surprised by it. The scent of cooking meat accompanied by the sound of laughter wafted over Rawley when he exited the truck, and he followed his senses to the back of the house. He leaned a shoulder against the corner of the house to peek around. He needed to assess the situation he would be interrupting before he announced his arrival.

Sylvia swayed lazily in the porch swing while Ryan flipped slabs of meat on the grill. Case's ex-boyfriend and Trent, the clerk from the hotel across from the station, sat beside Jake on the steps of the porch talking and laughing. Rawley was disappointed that Case was nowhere in sight.

Chapter Nineteen

CASE WAS IN the kitchen, spooning potato salad into a bowl, when the familiar rumble of Rawley's truck reached his ears, growing louder as it came down the drive. He still hadn't figured out his feelings over Rawley's sudden disappearance, so he stood there, listening to Rawley get closer and trying to decide which emotion he would settle on. Was he happy to see the sheriff? Angry that Rawley had just walked away? Grateful the damn man had come back? He didn't know.

Serious relationships had never been a part of his life, but he was fairly certain that one partner taking off for a week without warning wasn't how it supposed to work. Except, Case wasn't even dating Rawley, let alone in a relationship with him. They were just two men who'd been through hell and were trying to find their way to a new normal.

Case was jerked out of his stupor when the truck engine cut off, followed by the heavy metal door slamming shut. He leaned to the side, glancing through the screen door to see if the others were aware they had another guest. Aunt Sylvia looked over her shoulder at him and winked before returning her attention to the activity going on in front of her. Jake was animatedly telling Trent and Jordan about some hunting trip he'd been on when he'd come across a bear. Ryan somehow managed to grill the ribs all while staring at his partner with an expression of pure adoration.

Sighing heavily, he put the utensils down and headed for the front door to let Rawley in. When he stepped out onto the porch, the sheriff was nowhere to be seen. Knowing the truck hadn't driven itself to the house, Case left the porch to investigate. He stopped in front of his Mustang, hands on hips, wondering where the hell the man had gone in such a short amount of time. Conversation from the back of the house could be heard, so he moved around the side, suspecting Rawley would have followed the sound of voices.

His heart thundered in his chest at the sight of Rawley, leaning against the back corner of the house, peeking around it like a thief. Damn, he'd missed this gorgeous man. Case had thought the uniform was hot, that jeans paired with a button-down had been droolworthy, but Rawley in hiking boots, dirt-encrusted jeans, and a skintight white T-shirt inspired an erection. Or maybe it was just the six days without seeing the man causing Case to grow painfully hard. Case approached Rawley slowly, not wanting to startle him. He had no idea why the man was lurking in the shadows, instead of announcing his presence, but Case took advantage of the moment to admire the sheriff's fine ass and muscular back while he moved closer, until Rawley pressed back against the wall to face him. All the mixed-up emotions he had suffered through the past week dissipated like fog under the heat of Rawley's gaze.

"Hey there, beautiful," Rawley said quietly.

"Welcome home," Case responded, just as softly.

Rawley smiled, but his face was creased in a worried expression, those brown eyes questioning. It was nice to know he wasn't the only one uncertain about how to feel or at a loss as to what to do next. Rawley shoved his hands into his pockets and looked down at his feet with a shake of his head. Case closed the few feet of distance between them and slipped his arms around Rawley's waist, resting his cheek on Rawley's shoulder.

"I missed you," Case whispered against the skin of Rawley's neck.

"God, I missed you, too, Casey."

Rawley circled Case's body in a tight embrace, and then traced a line up Case's spine, eliciting a shiver, to cup the back of his head where he threaded his fingers through his hair. Case pulled back enough to nibble at Rawley's full bottom lip. Rawley groaned in response and fisted both hands in Case's hair, pressing their foreheads together with a ragged chuckle.

"Casey, the things you do to me," Rawley murmured and kissed the tip of Case's nose. "I'd like to take you out to dinner, give us a chance to talk and get to know each other."

"Yeah? Out...like...in public?"

"Yes, in public."

"But—" Case started.

"I won't hide you, Casey. I have my doubts and insecurities about us being right for each other, but I'll never deny you."

"Okay," Case breathed as he went soft in Rawley's arms.

He had no idea what had happened in the last week that had taken Rawley from not being ready for a relationship to openly dating him, but that was a conversation for another time. Rawley moved his hands from Case's hair to his cheeks and brushed his mouth lightly across Case's lips.

"I came here with the best intentions," Rawley whispered. "But then you get that dreamy look in your eyes and all I want to do is get you naked beneath me."

Case fisted the T-shirt at Rawley's lower back, smiling mischievously. "You know, some of the most honest conversations I've had were after very athletic and satisfying sex. Nothing like an intense orgasm to exhaust the pretense right out of you."

Rawley released his face so he could put some space between their bodies after Case rolled his hips suggestively, but Rawley didn't let go of him completely. He continued to grip Case's elbows, his thumbs making tiny circles over the exposed skin. The tenderness of the caress sent shivers through Case's body.

"You have company," Rawley said.

"I know, which is why dinner has to wait, but we could have a quickie in the bed of your truck," Case suggested, feeling daring. He didn't actually expect Rawley to drag him to the truck, but he held onto a tiny hope that Rawley would show more of his caveman tendencies. Case found it hot. Rawley looked in the direction of his truck, like he was truly considering it, and Case's heart skipped a beat.

Rawley scrubbed a hand down his face. "Don't tempt me."

He took Case's hand in his, linking their fingers, and led Case to the backyard where the others waited. Rawley stopped walking, his grip tightening, when he saw everyone seated around the wrought-iron table set up on the back porch. Two empty chairs sat side by side, place settings in front of each.

"What is it?" Case asked, pressing his chest against Rawley's upper arm.

"Were you expecting someone else?" Rawley stared at the empty chairs in confusion.

"No, but I'm sure they heard you arrive and pulled out another chair. Rawley," Case murmured, nibbling along the shell of Rawley's ear. "You can hear that truck of yours a mile away." Case started walking, pulling Rawley along by the hand.

"We went in the kitchen and got the rest of the food finished up, since someone decided to abandon his duties," Jake said with a wink.

"Thanks," Case said as he climbed the three steps and walked around the table to the empty chairs. He was about to sit next to Jordan when Rawley changed his trajectory, pushing him into the other chair, next to Ryan. Case chuckled at the possessiveness Rawley was exhibiting and basked in the joy the display elicited as Rawley claimed his seat at the table.

Chapter Twenty

RAWLEY CHOKED DOWN the flare of jealousy, but did nothing to hide the possessiveness as he steered Case away from the chair beside his ex. He didn't know the guy personally, but if he was sitting at a table with Ryan, Jake, and Sylvia, then he must have some redeeming quality. It didn't make a difference, though. Rawley still didn't want him around Case. Unfortunately, he had no control over where this man went or what he did, so Rawley would settle for being a wall between the two. Rawley rested his hand on Case's thigh under the table, squeezing gently, and earning a broad smile from his man.

"I'm so glad you decided to join us, Rawley," Sylvia said from across the table.

Case continued to beam at Rawley, leaned against him slightly, and said, "Yeah, thanks for showing."

Rawley held Case's gray-blue gaze for a long moment. Those few words were laced with hidden meaning. Rawley rubbed the tip of his nose across Case's in a quick caress, squeezing his thigh again and ignoring the five sets of eyes watching them in surprise. It was the first intimate moment they'd shared openly, but the anxiety Rawley had expected to feel never happened. Instead, he felt calm, free, and rapidly falling for the young man who was idly drawing patterns on the back of his hand where it sat on his thigh.

"Well, everyone, feel free to dig in before the food gets cold," Sylvia said, effectively pulling the attention back to the dinner set out on the table.

Without argument, they began passing around plates of ribs and sausages, baskets of rolls, and bowls of salad. Sylvia's musical laughter stopped the activity around the table as they all focused on her.

"What's funny?" Jake asked from his spot beside her.

"Eddie would be so amused by this. Instead of gossiping with other women my age down at the salon, I'm sitting at a table with six handsome, young gay men eating sausages."

Case blushed furiously. "Jeez, Aunt Sylvia," he muttered, as the entire table erupted into laughter. Rawley had never realized the woman had such a dirty sense of humor, but then he couldn't remember the last time he had socialized with her, or anyone from town, in a nonprofessional manner. It was something he had no doubt would change with Case in his life. The man was a social butterfly just like his aunt.

The laughter died down until everyone fell silent as they turned their attention to the food. Even Sylvia seemed content to sit quietly and enjoy a meal shared with good company. Rawley was acutely aware every time the ex-boyfriend glanced at Case, and Rawley caught his own attention drifting toward Case regularly. It seemed every move he made was erotic, specifically designed to drive Rawley out of his mind. His dick had gone stiff the second Case had idly sucked barbecue sauce off a finger, and it had been throbbing in his pants ever since. After he'd cleaned his plate, Rawley draped an arm across the back of Case's chair, lazily playing with the dark strands of hair at the nape of his neck as he relaxed. Once he started touching his beautiful man, he didn't want to stop.

"I didn't know you were gay, Sheriff Kane," Trent said softly, a light blush pinking up his cheeks.

Rawley smiled at the young hotel clerk before sweeping his gaze around the table to find everyone's attention was back on the two of them. Jake and Trent watched him inquisitively, Sylvia's expression was a mixture of pleasure and love, mostly directed at Case, but Ryan and the ex both looked annoyed. The ex Rawley could understand, but Ryan's reaction was confusing so he made a mental note to ask him about it later.

"Never had a reason to make it known," Rawley responded and then turned to look Case in the eye. "Until now."

"Where have you been the past week?" Ryan asked, glaring daggers at Rawley from the other side of Case.

Rawley had no idea how to take the man's sudden animosity. Ryan was practically married to Jake. It would be hypocritical of him to have a problem with Rawley being gay, so it had to be something else. He just didn't know what it could be. Case was confused as well if the glare he gave Ryan was any indication. Rawley kissed Case's temple and then answered honestly, albeit cryptically. The details of his psychological housecleaning were reserved solely for the man who incited the desire to change.

"I went back to Denver. Put some old ghosts to rest."

Case's expression immediately changed to one of understanding as he buried his face in Rawley's neck. He was the only one at the table who knew about Alex and all the pain associated with his loss, so he was also the only one to know the significance of the trip. Sylvia steered the topic of conversation to Trent's college education, which he continued to put off. Eventually things grew more relaxed. The only person who didn't seem to be enjoying the early evening Sunday quiet and the present company was Case's ex-boyfriend. Rawley was getting tired of thinking of the guy as an ex. He would have to ask Case what the dude's name was, but not right now. He was taking too much pleasure rubbing it in the guy's face that Case had chosen a small-town sheriff as the recipient of his affection rather than a rich pretty-boy socialite.

A couple of hours later, and several not-so-subtle touches, Sylvia announced that she was tired. While the sun sank behind the trees, slowly disappearing behind the distant mountains, they all set about helping clean up. Ryan returned to the grill, while Jake took the chairs to a corner of the porch where he stacked them. Trent busied himself wiping down the table. Rawley and the ex-boyfriend picked up dishes to carry into the kitchen so Case could package the leftovers for storage. The entire time Rawley received angry glares, to which he just smiled, enjoying the hell out of the interaction. Case passed empty dishes to Sylvia, who rinsed them before loading them into the dishwasher. In a matter of minutes, the place was clean. Everyone gathered in the kitchen, ready to say their goodbyes and head home.

"Gentlemen, thank you for the lovely afternoon," Sylvia said. "I know it's early, but I'm heading to bed with a good book. Good night."

She hugged everyone goodbye and kissed Case on the cheek before disappearing down the hall to her bedroom. Jake and Trent said their goodbyes to the rest of the group and walked through the living room toward the door. Rawley watched the ex-boyfriend sidle closer to Case who stood by the sink. When Rawley moved to intercept, Ryan stopped him by grabbing his upper arm and shoving him out the back door onto the porch. Ryan released him only long enough to push against his chest and slam his back against the house.

"What the fuck is your problem?" Rawley said as he shoved Ryan back. "You have been mean mugging me since I got here."

Ryan got right in his face. "I don't give a shit that Case has forgiven you. If you ever do that to him again, I'll knock your goddamned teeth out, sheriff or not."

That was a decidedly more intimate threat than Ryan had a right to make, considering he was with Jake, and the thought of Ryan and Case together made Rawley angry enough to get back in Ryan's face.

"If I find out you touched him…"

"Don't give me that. I'm not the one who fucked him and then abandoned him for a week without a word."

Ryan's words calmed Rawley. "You don't know the whole story. He does. He understands what I did and why," Rawley said. "At least he does now. I should have told him I was leaving for a bit, but he understands why I had to do it."

Ryan narrowed his eyes and took a few steps back at Rawley's unexpected smile. He was elated that Case had made friends in Clover City because maybe, just maybe, it meant he wasn't planning on leaving anytime soon. He wasn't sure how he felt about Case sharing their sex life with Ryan, which meant he'd also shared it with Jake, but that was a minor thing compared to knowing Case had support here.

"I'm falling in love with him," Rawley confided, and watched the remainder of Ryan's anger recede.

Ryan sighed. He ran a hand through his hair as he motioned to the house. "You better get back inside and tell him that. Jordan has been getting more insistent lately, and Trent has made his interest known, too."

Ryan took the porch steps two at a time before disappearing around the corner of the house, heading for the vehicles parked around front. Ryan called out for Trent to hop into the truck so they could take him home. Rawley took a deep, steadying breath, preparing to go to battle for his man. At least he had a name for the ex now—Jordan.

Chapter Twenty-One

IT HAD BEEN impossible for him to ignore the longing looks Jordan and Trent sent in Case's direction. He wondered if Case would have given in to one, or both, of them if he'd continued to resist Case's desires. Trent had sent Jordan a few glances as well, but those had been hotter, more lustful, and he felt bad for the kid if things had gotten sexual. Especially if Jordan really was as shallow and greedy as Case had made him sound. Steeling his nerves for what he might walk in on, Rawley reentered the house. Following the sound of raised voices to Ed's den, he pressed his ear to the door to hear Case and Jordan fighting.

"What part of that don't you get?" Case shouted. Rawley realized the two men were arguing so loudly he didn't need to have his ear against the door so he stepped back.

"You forget how well I know you. I've been to your parties. Drugs, alcohol, sex. Christ, the last party you threw you were fucking me, Garrett, and Parker simultaneously. One man isn't enough for you. Never has been," Jordan yelled back.

"Just go home," Case said, his tone tired, pleading.

"Fine. Fuck the cop all you want, but you'll get tired of him. He'll just be another Richard because eventually you're going to need more than one dick and when you do, you know where to find us."

Rawley's gut twisted as his fledgling happiness took a hit of doubt. Jordan made it sound like Case had commitment issues, that monogamy was something he couldn't do. Ready for their conversation to end, and more than ready for Jordan to be on his way, Rawley opened the door without knocking, walking in on the last thing he ever wanted to see. He closed his eyes and swallowed, forcing his breathing to remain even. Jordan had Case pressed against the wall beside the fireplace with his tongue in Case's mouth. Once his anger was somewhat controlled, Rawley opened his eyes to find Case had broken free of Jordan's hold and was watching Rawley closely.

"Was it unwanted?" Rawley asked.

"Yes, but it's fine. He's leaving." Case looked to Jordan. "Aren't you." Case's tone suggested it wasn't a question, but a firm suggestion.

"Yeah. Don't have kittens there, Sheriff. I was just reminding our man what my mouth and tongue can do."

"He's not *our* man. He's *my* man and don't even think about touching him again," Rawley said as Jordan passed him on the way out the door. He wanted to punch the smug smile off Jordan's face.

"Get used to it. You'll always be sharing him. If not with me, then someone else. There will always be other men."

Rawley barely waited until Jordan cleared the doorframe before he slammed the door shut in his face. He was seething. That man had not only forced his attentions on Case, but then he turned around and suggested that Rawley would never be able to keep Case. He pressed his forehead to the door, listening to Sylvia and Jordan exchange words while he reined his temper in. He didn't want to scare Case or take his fury out on him. Rawley felt the soft knock even as the dull thud reached his ears.

"Are you okay, Casey?" Sylvia called through the door.

Rawley turned to face the room. Case was seated on the sofa with his face in his hands, his shoulders hunched. He looked exhausted and beat down.

Case dropped his hands only to stare into the fire. "I'm fine, Aunt Sylvia. Sorry we disturbed you."

"You know where to find me if you need to talk," Sylvia said.

Her footsteps retreated as Case breathed out a "Thanks."

Rawley joined him on the couch, touching him from thigh to shoulder, because he had to have contact at this moment. He wrapped an arm around Case's shoulders and hugged him close to his body. Rawley was a jumbled mess of nerves and emotions, and he imagined Case was the same, so he simply held him in silence. Case canted his head sideways to rest it on Rawley's shoulder.

"I put the house up for sale," Case said.

"What house?" Rawley asked, confused by the odd topic.

"My house in Denver. You spent the last week putting your past to rest. I just wanted you to know I was doing the same."

"Casey—"

"I don't cheat," Case interrupted. It was another odd comment that threw Rawley. "I mean I did, but I didn't mean to."

Rawley didn't know how a person could cheat without being aware of it, so he mumbled an "Okay" and waited for Case to elaborate.

"This one guy, Richard, thought we were exclusive boyfriends. I gave him a key to the house and he misunderstood, took it to mean more than was intended. I had given all the men I fucked on a regular basis a key. It didn't mean anything, at least not to me. He came over one day and saw me with Landon." Case sighed, shaking his head slightly against Rawley's shoulder, the soft tendrils of his hair tickling Rawley's jaw. "Looking back, I can see what an asshole I was. How I completely ignored all the signs that he was attached and treated him like shit, completely discounting all of his feelings. At the time, I thought he was overreacting, but now..."

Case pushed away from Rawley, launched to his feet, and began pacing the small room. Rawley had witnessed Case's high energy level before, but it had always been positive. He hadn't known Case was capable of this level of irritated frustration. He wanted to offer comfort, but instead he remained silent and followed Case with his gaze as he moved from the fireplace to the window and back again repeatedly. The argument with Jordan must have opened a wound Case had tried to keep closed. Rawley was content to wait while Case purged.

"My grandfather died of cancer when I was nineteen and left me a shit ton of money, made me a millionaire overnight. I own an expensive house, drive a nice car. I have everything I could ever want, and what do I do? I go stupid and become a drunken, partying slut. I fuck every man who shows interest, simply because I hate being alone. I'm not sure coming here solved anything because all it did was give me time to think and help me realize how self-centered, shallow, spoiled—"

"No, you're not," Rawley interrupted softly. He didn't want this beautiful young man he was growing to love thinking so badly of himself.

"—and pathetic I am," Case finished with only slightly less conviction.

Rawley shook his head, watching Case come to a stop in front of the window to look out at the inky blackness. He thumped his forehead against the glass and let out a shuddering sigh. Rawley joined Case at the window, stood behind him, and bracketed Case with his arms, hands against the glass. He eliminated all distance between their bodies, pressing his pelvis against Case's ass. Case's eyes fluttered closed, but he remained still, allowing Rawley to surround him.

"You weren't in love with any of them?" Rawley asked.

"No," Case whispered.

"How often did you have sex when you were this drinking, partying slut?"

"All the time…daily, nightly…whatever. There was always someone who wanted me. I was fucking six men if you remember."

"I remember." Rawley kissed the shell of Case's ear. "Over the past couple of weeks, since you got here, how often do you have sex? How many men are you with now?"

Case turned in Rawley's arms and cupped his cheeks, their faces a mere inch apart. His distress was clear in his stormy gray-blue eyes.

"Only you, I swear. There's only you…"

Rawley stopped his words with a soul-stealing kiss. He hadn't meant for the line of questioning to sound accusatory, but Case's reaction suggested that's how it was taken. Given Case's self-deprecating line of thinking, it wasn't surprising. Reluctantly, Rawley pulled out of the kiss, but he stayed pressed against Case's body because he couldn't bear the thought of not touching Case in this moment.

"I wasn't suggesting you were sleeping around or reverting to your old ways. I'm trying to point out how you've changed since you arrived. You're not the same man here that you were in Denver. You're not fucking every man who shows interest, or Jordan wouldn't have left in a rage, and Trent wouldn't have gone all sullen at dinner when it became clear we were together."

"Trent just has a crush, but are we together? Officially?" Case asked.

Rawley braced his weight on one hand against the window glass so he could thread his fingers through Case's thick, dark hair. "Yes, I think that's what we both want," Rawley murmured against Case's lips.

Case nodded and hugged Rawley around the waist. "It is." He nuzzled beneath Rawley's ear. "Come to bed with me," he whispered, sliding a hand down over the curve of Rawley's ass.

"Hell, no." Rawley disengaged from Case's arms. He took several steps back, but Case followed, refusing to let Rawley retreat. "Casey, we are not having sex in this house. Sylvia is in the room directly across from yours, and maybe you don't remember, but sex between us is very loud."

"I don't remember that at all. You might need to give me a long, hard reminder," Case said.

Rawley started to speak, but Case's tongue invaded his mouth, his toned body rubbing against Rawley in a way certain to make him come in his jeans. Rawley gave in for a few minutes, sucking on Case's tongue, nibbling at his lips, pushing his own tongue into Case's mouth in a fight for dominance. He was lost to the sensations as his head was filled with the intoxicating flavor and scent of his gorgeous, young lover. It was the pressure of Case wrapping a leg around his hip and rutting against his thigh that snapped Rawley back to their surroundings. They would end up fucking on the floor if he didn't put a stop to their play, because Case was damn persuasive. Rawley pulled out of the kiss and gave Case's butt cheek a hard, open-palmed swat.

"Not here, Casey." Rawley took Case's hand in his and lifted it to his lips where he trailed kisses over the knuckles before adding, "Come home with me."

"Okay."

Case's smile was wide, so stunningly beautiful in that moment with his eyes clouded with lust, his hair in disarray. Rawley squeezed his hand as he pulled Case behind him to the front door, desperate now to get his lover to the house, naked, and in bed. At Case's insistence, Rawley waited on the front porch in the cooling, humid evening air while Case shut off lights and let his aunt know he was leaving with Rawley. When Case joined him on the porch, turning his back to lock the door, Rawley embraced him from behind and kissed his neck.

Holding Case against him, he shuffled them across the porch to the steps, where he was forced to let go so they could safely descend the steps. Case laughed the entire time he practically skipped to the passenger side of the truck. When he reached for the door handle, Rawley spun him and pressed him back against the cab. Two hot, stolen, tongue-filled kisses later, Rawley dodged around the hood of the truck to climb in beside Case.

As he maneuvered the truck over the rutted drive to the highway, Rawley watched Case surreptitiously and did his best to stay at the speed limit. It was difficult not to feel rushed and impatient, especially with Case sitting next to him, bouncing his leg with pent-up energy while he stared out the side window in silence. The pensive expression concerned Rawley a bit, making him anxious, so he reached over to squeeze Case's firm thigh, just above the knee. He wanted his happy, carefree boyfriend back.

"Casey, are you okay? We don't have to do this—have sex. I'll just hold you all night if that's what you want."

Case shook his head but continued to stare out the window at the darkened landscape. "I want it." He placed his hand on top of Rawley's, where it rested on his leg. "It's just when you disappeared... I thought it was because you decided you didn't want me."

Case spoke the words softly, but Rawley felt the barb the same as if Case had screamed at him, and it hurt to know he'd caused Case emotional distress. The conversation with Ryan on the back porch suddenly made sense. During the drive home from Denver, Rawley had wondered if Case would feel worry or anger over him going AWOL for a week. It had never occurred to him that Case might feel rejected. Rawley was no longer annoyed that Case had spoken about their activities together. Instead, he was grateful Case had taken his heartache to Jake and Ryan rather than to Jordan's or Trent's bed.

"I've always wanted you, Casey, from the minute I laid eyes on you. And I promise you, here and now, that I'll never take off like that again. I hate that I hurt you."

"I wasn't hurt, exactly, just extremely confused. I knew you'd be back eventually, and we'd have a chance to figure it out."

"Yeah. The need to get back to home and work aside, I couldn't stay away from you for long. I started itching to get back to you sometime Monday, and it only grew stronger every day."

Chapter Twenty-Two

RAWLEY PARKED THE truck in his driveway feeling immediate relief. It felt good to be home, and even better to have Case there with him. They both got out of the cab, and Rawley pulled his travel bag from behind the seat while Case walked to the front door. He leaned against the house, waiting patiently, but the look he leveled on Rawley as Rawley joined him at the door had Rawley's dick plumping in anticipation. Feeling just as desperate as Case looked, he took Case's mouth in a rough kiss, which Case returned with unbridled enthusiasm.

He never wanted to stop kissing Case, but he did want to get him in the house so they could get down to the business of loving on each other, so he pulled Case into his side while he unlocked the front door. When it swung open, he walked Case backward into the house, nipping once at his lips before he released him to relock the door and turn on the table lamp. He decided that the mood called more for softer lighting rather than the brightness of the overhead fixture. A warm glow illuminated the room as Case pressed his chest to Rawley's back and embraced him from behind, pumping his erection against Rawley's ass.

Taking one of Case's hands in his, Rawley pulled him around to the front of his body where he spun Case a couple of times. Case twirled in place, laughing, before he lost his balance. Rawley took advantage, pushing Case backward onto the sofa, following him down to settle between his legs. Case hooked his ankles around Rawley's hips. He threaded his fingers through Rawley's hair as Rawley lay him down and balanced with one knee pressed snuggly against the inside of Case's thigh on the cushion. He used the foot on the floor as leverage to buck his hips, rubbing their jean-covered cocks together roughly while he feasted on Case's mouth.

It had only been six days, but he had truly missed this man. Rawley brushed Case's dark hair away from his forehead and buried his face in Case's neck while Case's hands took a trip down his back to grab the hem of his shirt, pulling it up so he could get at Rawley's bare skin. Shivers raced through his body and escalated his excitement to the point that he either needed to disengage from his man, allow himself time to calm down a bit, or get inside him now.

Rawley lifted to an elbow so he could look into Case's eyes. "Sex or talk?"

"Seriously?" Case grated out.

"Right, sex first, but we *will* talk after."

Case moaned in agreement as Rawley slipped a hand between their bodies to palm Case's erection. He gave a gentle squeeze, and then proceeded to open Case's jeans with urgent, uncoordinated moves. They eventually managed to get Case's pants and boxer shorts down around his thighs, freeing his rigid shaft. Rawley stayed close, forcing the fabric to bunch beneath the globes of Case's ass, because he didn't want to stop touching, yet. He kissed the exposed skin of Case's neck, sucked on the lobe of Case's ear, nipping at the soft flesh.

Case's response was a groan accompanied by an upward thrust of his hips, searching for contact, but his jeans kept their bodies from connecting fully. It was both exhilarating and frustrating, and perfectly clear they were both ready. Rawley pushed up on one knee while working Case's jeans and underwear off. He backed away only far enough to pull the clothing free, tossed them to the floor, and then quickly returned to the cradle of Case's thighs, acutely aware he was still fully dressed. Case didn't seem to mind. He continued to play under Rawley's shirt, tweaking his nipples and dragging his blunt nails over his pecs.

"I want easier access to your ass," Rawley murmured into the ear he'd been sucking on. Case panted an indecipherable affirmative that made Rawley smile. It was a boost to his ego that he could make his younger lover speechless without even being inside him.

"Get on your knees," Rawley said as he moved off Case's body. He expected Case to roll over, but instead, he moved to the floor and bent over the sofa. Case turned his head on the seat cushion to look up at Rawley.

"Fuck me, right here, just like this."

Rawley adjusted himself in his jeans as he took a moment to soak in his lover's appearance. The man was gorgeous, with messy dark hair framing his face, and lust-filled eyes silently begging for Rawley to give him what he needed. Rawley took hold of Case's hand as he stood up from the couch and circled around to stand behind Case. He used one booted foot to nudge Case's knees farther apart, spreading his legs wide enough for Rawley to kneel between them.

He massaged the smooth, round butt cheeks, occasionally pulling the globes apart to watch Case's pucker spasm. Case rocked back and forth slightly, probably to add a little friction to his cock pressed against the edge of the sofa. Rawley held Case open, leaned down to flick his tongue across the star, and then lightly blew across the damp skin. Case jerked at the hot/cold sensation, so Rawley repeated the action a few times until Case breathlessly begged him for more. Giving in to the request, Rawley set about giving Case the rimming of his life, occasionally darting his tongue inside, drowning in his lover's taste and the sound of his gasping moans.

"More...more," Case panted as he pushed harder against Rawley's face.

Rawley wet two fingers in his mouth, pressed them to the pucker in a circular motion, and gently worked the digits past the tight ring of muscle until Case's body relaxed around them allowing Rawley to push them deeper. Case slapped open palms onto the cushion with a loud intake of breath. Both men held still while Case adjusted. Rawley waited, enraptured as he watched Case fuck himself on Rawley's fingers. He rotated his hand with every backward thrust of Case's hips until he once again rendered the man mute. When he could no longer hold back his own pleasure, he pulled his fingers free.

"Are you going to fuck me now, Rawley?"

"Yes, beautiful, I am."

Rawley folded over Case's back and bit his shoulder through his shirt, causing Case to jerk beneath him with a gasp. Rawley briefly wondered if he'd bitten too hard, but undulating hips put that concern to rest. Case's shirt clung to his back, sweaty from the heat pouring off his body. Rawley threaded his fingers through the damp hair at the base of Case's neck as he dragged his other hand down the length of Case's spine. He pumped his jean-clad erection against the exposed, sensitized skin of Case's ass, rocking him into the sofa. Case reached back with both hands and gripped Rawley's thighs tightly.

"You have to stop before I come. I want you in me first."

Rawley immediately pulled back and released his lover. He wanted to be inside Case when he came, too. It would be nice if he could manage to make them both come together, but he wasn't sure he would succeed. He was damn well going to try, though. Rubbing Case's calf with one hand, Rawley dug into his pocket for the condom and packet of lube he'd stashed there earlier. He tossed the items on the floor by Case's ankle, opened his jeans, and shoved them to his knees. Not wanting to lose any of the arousal he'd achieved, Rawley kissed the exposed, slightly damp skin of Case's lower back as he quickly covered himself and slicked up. He used the excess lube on Case's taint, smiling in satisfaction at the yelp of surprise it elicited from his young man.

"Open yourself for me," Rawley urged.

He licked his lips in anticipation as Case buried his face in the cushion as he spread his butt cheeks to offer an unobstructed path to his hot spot. Rawley held Case's hip, pressed the tip of his cock against Case's entrance, and then slowly pushed in until he felt the ring of muscle give and he slid home. Once he was completely seated, hips snug against Case's upturned ass, he wrapped his arms around Case's middle, holding him while they both regained some semblance of control. Neither of them wanted it to be over too quickly, though once Rawley started moving, it would be a mad dash for the finish line. He only hoped they'd cross together. Rawley kissed and licked every inch of Case's body he could comfortably reach as the tight grip surrounding his cock relaxed a bit.

Case straightened off the couch, pushing Rawley back on his heels, until his weight rested on Rawley's thighs. He reached behind him and threaded his fingers through Rawley's hair as he tipped his head back onto Rawley's shoulder. That tight little ass clenched spasmodically around Rawley's cock overwhelming him with the need to thrust. Slipping a hand under Case's shirt, he pressed his palm against hot skin, holding him firmly as he wrapped his other hand around Case's shaft to stroke him. Case wiggled his hips and Rawley couldn't hold back any longer. He began with slow, shallow upward thrusts until they both needed hard, fast, and deep.

Rawley folded Case back over the sofa, grabbed Case's hips in both hands, and fucked into him with barely controlled force. The sight of his length moving in and out of his lover held him spellbound until he felt the tingling of impending orgasm racing down his spine, tightening his balls. He wrapped himself around Case's body so he could stroke his dick as he drilled his ass. Case covered Rawley's hand with his own, helping Rawley work him the way he needed.

"Rawley, fuck, yes," Case screamed into the cushion, the padding muffling his cries of release as he shot his load onto their joined hands and the floor.

Several hard thrusts later, Rawley came, buried to the hilt in Case's body. He pumped his hips once and froze, immediately noticing the fluid leaking out around his shaft. He sat back on his heels, bringing Case with him because he wasn't ready to separate their bodies yet, and buried his face in Case's neck. Silently, he cursed faulty condoms.

"Holy, shit, that was just so...fucking amazing," Case breathed.

"I came inside you," Rawley mumbled, lips brushing over Case's damp skin.

Case squeezed the back of Rawley's sweaty neck. "Mm, yes, you did."

"The condom broke," Rawley added with a subtle shake of his head.

Case grabbed a fistful of Rawley's hair and pulled his head back so he could kiss Rawley's jaw. He rolled his hips, moving Rawley's semi-stiff dick inside him. The loud groan the action elicited from Case sent satisfaction coursing through him, but his shaft was overly sensitive, so he hugged Case tightly to still the movement. He canted his head to look at Rawley's face.

"I've never gone bare, not with anyone," he said. "And I get tested regularly. I'm clean. Given your years-long celibacy, I'm sure you are, too."

Rawley stared directly into Case's eyes as he whispered his admission. "I've never been tested."

"We can go get tested Monday. Make sure," Case offered.

"It would make me feel better." Case's smile was slow and lazy as he nodded. "My feet are going numb."

Case took Rawley's change of topic in stride, easing off Rawley's now-soft dick with a pained hiss. "Damn. Sore."

Rawley's regret morphed into renewed arousal as he watched his semen drip from Case's taint and slide down his thigh. He couldn't suppress the moan. Case glanced over his shoulder, lifting his brows in question.

"You're fucking hot like that. Bare-assed with my juice dripping out of you."

Case flopped to his back on the sofa, laughing and clearly satisfied. Rawley shifted on the floor to lean against the sofa, stretching his sore legs out in front of him. He brought Case's hand to his lips for a kiss before letting his head fall back onto Case's hip. Case squeezed his hand.

"Maybe someday I'll get to see what you look like with *my* juice dripping out of *you*."

Case's tone was sultry, suggestive, but fatigued. Rawley kissed the tip of Case's fingers again before releasing his hold so he could stand. They both needed a nap and Rawley knew from experience how uncomfortable the couch would become. His body protested every move as Rawley got to his feet, reminding him he was no longer as young as the man he'd just fucked. He grabbed Case's hands and pulled him to his feet. Case looked down and then started laughing, shaking his head.

"What?" Rawley asked as he looked down to see what Case had seen.

Rawley's pants were still around his knees, his T-shirt not long enough to conceal his flaccid dick. Case wore nothing more than his shirt and socks. Case walked to the kitchen to grab some paper towels while Rawley toed his hiking boots off so he could completely remove his pants. Case handed him a towel and they cleaned themselves.

"This is the second time we've had sex mostly dressed. I think I've forgotten what you look like naked," Case said.

He pulled Rawley's shirt off and then Rawley returned the favor. Case kissed him before heading to the bedroom wearing only socks. Rawley waited until he had entered the room and had the light turned on before he shut off the lamp and double-checked to make sure the front door was locked. It was a habit his mother had drilled into him as a child that he continued to do to this day. He found Case already under the covers waiting for him with sleepy eyes and a lazy smile. Returning the smile, Rawley shut the lights off and joined his boyfriend in the bed.

"You look happy," Case said as he snuggled against Rawley's side.

"I am," Rawley agreed as Case arranged himself across his chest. Hoping a sleepy, comfortable Case would be an uncensored Case, Rawley asked "How old are you, Casey?"

"You know, before I met you, I hated being called Casey. Now, I kind of like it." Case said as kissed Rawley's chest.

"Why did you hate it?"

"My parents, mostly. They don't like that I'm gay or that I inherited so much more money than they did. They always say my name with anger and derision. I preferred the shorter version my friends used, but that's changing because now I associate Case with the partying slut I used to be." Case moved over Rawley until he was draped fully over Rawley's upper body, his ear directly over Rawley's heart. Rawley wrapped his arms around him and kissed the top of Case's head. "Will you call me Casey all the time?"

"If you want, yes." Rawley massaged his lover's head and body until he feared Casey had fallen asleep. "Casey?"

"Mmmhmm?"

"How old are you?"

"Twenty-five," Casey answered sleepily; Rawley cringed. He'd known Casey was quite a bit younger than him, but not *that* much younger. He rubbed a hand over his face and groaned softly as Casey nosed beneath his ear. "You stiffened up. What's wrong?"

"I'm robbing the cradle. I don't have to worry about what people will think of me being gay because they'll be too focused on the fact I'm screwing a kid."

Casey nibbled along Rawley's jawline and sucked on his earlobe. "I'm not a kid, and you're not that much older than me, are you?"

Casey's lips on his skin were magic, sending tingles through his entire body. Rawley had to fight to keep his budding arousal in check.

"I'm forty-four," Rawley grated out while Casey worked his way down Rawley's neck. "Shit, I'm old enough to be your father."

"Actually," Casey said, lips now toying with one of Rawley's nipples. Rawley felt him smile as he circled the tightening bud with his tongue. "My dad is a couple of years younger than you."

Rawley's gut knotted and his chest constricted, making it hard to breathe as Casey's words sank in. He stared up at the darkened ceiling and concentrated on breathing normally. Intuitive as always, Casey picked up on his distress and blanketed Rawley with his body, faces close together. The man really was amazing.

"I'm so sorry. I wasn't insulting you or anything, honest. I just find it amusing," Casey assured him.

With firm, determined lips, Casey kissed Rawley, slipping his tongue inside as soon as Rawley opened for him. If distracting Rawley was what Casey had intended, he succeeded. The kiss was hot, wet, and so full of emotion it made Rawley's chest ache for an entirely different reason. Several moments later, Casey moved his scorching kisses back down to

Rawley's neck, over his shoulder, and Rawley was able to think again...kind of. Casey braced his legs around Rawley's hips as he shifted downward a bit.

He separated his lips from Rawley's skin long enough to murmur, "You're getting hard again. Want me to suck you off?"

"Yes! I mean, no." Rawley grabbed Casey beneath the arms and hauled him back over his chest when the man started to scoot down Rawley's legs to blow him. Casey gave a distressed noise. "Sorry. I would love to fill your mouth, but we can't be all about sex all the time. Stop trying to distract me and talk to me."

Casey sighed loudly before laying his head back on Rawley's chest, his body relaxed. "Doesn't it bother you that I'm so much older than you? Don't you want someone your own age who can keep up with you?"

"You've kept up just fine. And no, I don't want someone my age. I want you."

"I'm older than your parents—"

"Forget what I said about my parents," Casey interrupted. "They were teenagers when they had me, which was why I was with my grandfather so often. He pretty much raised me. I think that's why he left the majority of his wealth to me. My parents have always been irresponsible and immature, and for *me* to say that is pretty significant. I'm not saying I've been all that responsible and mature, either. In fact, I know I haven't, but at least I'm figuring my shit out in my twenties. They're in their damn forties, but still act like they're teenagers."

Casey lifted his face to kiss Rawley's chin while he adjusted on top of Rawley until he was comfortable. "Can we not talk about them anymore? They make me crazy. Besides, age doesn't matter when you're good together. And we are, aren't we? You're reserved and serious. I'm outgoing and loud."

"You're perfect," Rawley whispered into Casey's hair.

"You're the hot silver-fox cop, and I'm the cute, young troublemaker," Casey added making Rawley chuckle, despite his reservations.

"Cute, young, and loud, you are. Go to sleep, Casey."

Within moments, Casey was snoring softly in Rawley's arms. As Rawley drifted off, one thought became firmly implanted in his brain. Nineteen-year age difference be damned. He loved Casey Holden and he would do whatever it took to keep him in his life. He'd never be able to let him go now, anyway.

Chapter Twenty-Three

CASEY COULDN'T WIPE the stupid smile off his face, even when Rawley drove him back to his aunt's place. Not even the annoying texts, emails, and phone calls he continued to receive from all six exes, or the storm threatening to break any moment, was enough to deter his good mood. Rawley's truck rumbled to a stop behind the Mustang. Casey noted the absence of Aunt Sylvia's Jeep and then vaguely remembered her telling him she had a meeting with the social committee this morning. Casey was grateful for that. It meant he would have time to take care of his own crap and process everything without fielding a lot of questions.

He was already fishing his keys from his pocket when he hopped out of the truck. Rawley had to check in with his deputies and Casey had a list of things to get done before evening. His first stop would be the Cloverleaf Hotel for a no-holds-barred conversation with Jordan. Then he needed to contact the cell phone company to get his number changed. While Rawley had showered and dressed for work, Case had texted Parker, Derek, Garrett, Landon, and Brent to let them know he would not be returning to Denver. He'd used simple words to make it as clear as he possible he was no longer interested, but the sheer number of responses had forced him to turn the phone off. The last thing he wanted was for Rawley to hear how desperate Casey's ex-lovers were becoming. He had yet to turn the cell back on, afraid to see the number of missed calls and text messages he had received.

Eying the car, Casey wondered if he should keep it. It wasn't exactly practical for driving down Aunt Sylvia's driveway, especially in inclement weather, but he loved the Mustang Maybe he would just buy a Jeep or a big Ford pickup for when the weather was ugly. Of course, if he eventually got to live with Rawley, a higher clearance vehicle might not be necessary. Casey thought back over his life the past month and was shocked at how many big changes he had made without even being aware of it. The biggest being falling head over heels in love with Sheriff

Kane. As if knowing Casey's thoughts had centered on him, Rawley wrapped his arms around Casey's waist from behind and pulled him against his solid chest.

"I don't want to go to work," Rawley murmured.

"I don't want you to, either. You vanished for a week the last time I let you go."

Rawley spun him so they were facing each other and gazed unflinchingly into Casey's eyes. "That will never happen again. I promise you that."

Casey stared into those deep brown eyes and couldn't help but feel relieved at the sincerity behind the words. "I know. Go to work and I'll meet you at the station around six for dinner."

Rawley ran his hands over Case's short dark hair before leaning in to kiss him. They were weeks past due for a first date.

"Looking forward to it."

"Me, too."

Rawley kissed him again, this one lingering a bit longer, before releasing Casey and getting back into the truck. Casey spun his keys on a finger. He waved as Rawley turned the vehicle around and disappeared down the drive. The rumble of the truck engine slowly died out leaving Casey with his own thoughts. For the first time that morning, his smile slipped and the happiness edged into determination.

He pulled his cell phone from his pocket to turn it back on. Thunder rolled in the distance, the air growing humid with incoming rain. Casey couldn't help but think the storm was a physical manifestation of the turmoil he found himself mired in. The phone chimed, pulling his attention away from the darkening clouds overhead, and informing him he had eight voicemails as well as, holy shit, twenty-seven text messages.

Every single man had responded with emphatic disapproval, multiple times, with both phone calls and texts, to his "breaking up" with them. Casey couldn't figure that out. It's not like they had ever dated in the first place, so how could he break up with them? Visiting his aunt in Clover City, and subsequently meeting Rawley and falling for him, had irrevocably changed Casey for the better. In hindsight, he was able to see his relationships for what they were: nothing more than manipulation and empty sex. The environment had been toxic, slowly bleeding the life from him.

Fat drops of rain started falling so Casey quickly unlocked the Mustang and climbed into the driver's seat. He sat there for several long minutes, listening to the steady thump of heavy rain on the rooftop as he played every single voicemail, and then read every single text message, before deleting them all without responding. Every message had begun the same—they cared about him, missed him, needed him, only to become more venomous with each subsequent message. He scanned his list of contacts. Aside from Rawley, whose number he now had, and Aunt Sylvia, there was absolutely no one he wanted to stay in touch with.

After tossing the phone in the cup holder, he turned the ignition and lost himself for a moment in the gentle thrum of the engine. He tapped the gas pedal to emit the growl that never failed to make him smile. Casey would definitely be keeping the Mustang. It was just too sweet a ride to give up. He put the gearshift into drive and very carefully maneuvered the vehicle over the uneven terrain now reduced to with thick mud thanks to the rain.

Casey was fairly certain that Rawley would not have been pleased to learn he had plans to visit Jordan in his hotel room. Just mentioning Jordan's name made Rawley prickly, so Casey didn't even want to imagine what his lover's reaction would be to hearing Jordan's name in the same sentence as "hotel room." Instead, he'd chosen to tell Rawley he was running some errands, which wasn't entirely untrue. No doubt the guilt would have him spilling his guts about the omission over dinner tonight. Plus, there was no real way to hide his bright-gold Mustang. If Rawley left the station or looked out the window, he would see it parked in front of the Cloverleaf Hotel. He just hoped that Rawley would understand the need for Casey to sever all ties with his past.

He angled the car onto the highway just as the clouds released a torrent of rain, dropping visibility substantially, even with the headlights on and the wipers going full speed. Casey thought back to the driveway he'd just barely been able to drive on in the soft rain and once again went over the pros and cons of owning a four-wheel drive vehicle when the ringing of his phone drew his attention. He activated the screen with a swipe of his thumb. Parker was calling for the third time that morning.

Case released the phone, but missed the cup holder and the phone fell to the floor by his foot. He pursed his lips and blew out a frustrated breath. The amazing happiness he'd held onto all morning was rapidly morphing into annoyance. When he finally reached Jordan, he was going to be primed for a fight. All six of his mistakes were proving to be relentless hardheads. Why wouldn't they just leave him alone? Yes, he had money, but plenty of people did. These guys would have no problem finding someone else to bankroll them, and none of them would have a problem finding another man to screw. He slammed his palm against the steering wheel when the phone rang from the floorboard.

"Fucking hell, why can't you just go away?" Casey shouted to the cosmos.

Temper snapping, Casey bent sideways to reach down along his leg for the phone. He shifted his foot off the gas pedal slightly so he could bend that little bit farther and wrap his fingers around the cell. He snagged it with two fingers and straightened in the seat. He had only looked away from the road for a few seconds, but he found the guardrail framing Willow Creek Bridge directly in front of him, and his heart stopped in his chest.

"Shit!"

Forgetting the phone, allowing it to clatter to the floorboard again, Casey gripped the wheel with both hands to jerk the Mustang hard to the left, back onto the pavement. He managed to avoid colliding with wood and steel, but the heavy rain had created another hazard he hadn't considered. The Mustang's tires lost grip and the vehicle hydroplaned out of control, skipping across the wet pavement in a spin at over fifty miles per hour. Casey knew he was in trouble but didn't have time to truly comprehend what was happening before the front wheel slammed into the railing on the other side of the paved bridge. The sudden hit combined with speed caused the Mustang to go off the road on the other side of the highway, before it flipped and rolled down the steep hill toward the creek. The car came to an abrupt, bone-breaking stop on its roof, half submerged in the rain-swollen waters of Willow Creek.

Chapter Twenty-Four

RAWLEY RUBBED HIS eyes and then slapped his cheeks in an attempt to wake himself up. Paperwork was the nemesis of every cop; made that much harder when said cop was exhausted from a night spent fooling around with his boyfriend, rather than actually sleeping. Rawley was a lucky man to have won the heart of young man like Casey Holden, and he would happily face a lifetime of fatigue-filled days if it meant Casey was in his arms every night. There were still a few hurdles they had to navigate around, namely Jordan and the other men Casey was leaving behind.

Rawley had watched Casey send the "I'm not coming back" text to all six men at once before leaving his lover in bed to shower that morning. He wasn't naïve enough to believe any of them took kindly to such a message. Casey had been in a great mood, hadn't once looked at his phone while Rawley was in his presence, but he knew Casey would be dealing with the fallout the rest of the day. Especially when one of them was still in town.

Jordan's sleek Corvette had still been parked in the lot of the Cloverleaf Hotel when Rawley had arrived at the station. It irked him. If Jordan was sticking around for Trent, fine. But if he was hanging around to pester Casey about getting back together, Rawley would be having a conversation with the man.

Rawley tamped down the urge to march across the street to have that conversation now, instead returning his attention to the paperwork that had been neglected during his week off. The murmured voices of his deputies were a comforting soundtrack that eased his stress and helped him focus. In just a few short hours, he would be sitting across the table from Casey, eating steak, drinking wine, and simply enjoying one another's company. It would be their first official date. It would also be the first time Rawley would show the town he was a gay man in love.

"Kane," Ted shouted seconds before the man himself showed up in the door of Rawley's office.

Ted's expression was all Rawley needed to see to know something serious had happened. Without a word, Ted turned and headed to the front door, with Rawley right on his heels. The rain continued to fall heavily, instantly soaking through their clothing. It reminded Rawley of the rainy day he'd met Casey, soaked to the skin, walking down the highway. Ted went to his four-wheel-drive Explorer, rather than Rawley's pickup that was clearly marked Sheriff. It was an unusual choice, but Rawley climbed into the passenger seat without argument.

"What happened?" Rawley asked as he snapped his seat belt in place.

Ted turned on the lights and siren even as he stepped on the accelerator. They left the parking lot in a spray of mud as the truck's wheels grabbed for purchase before launching onto the pavement. Additional sirens joined them and Rawley glanced at the side mirror to see a fire truck and an ambulance following behind.

"Trucker called saying there's a car on its roof in Willow Creek," Ted answered.

"Willow Creek. Not much out that way," Rawley said.

Except for Old Dave who ran a cattle ranch with his daughter and son-in-law, there was only Sylvia and Casey. He knew from experience that not many locals would go out in severe weather, knowing whatever they needed to do could wait. But not Casey. He was a city boy who was programmed to drive in any kind of weather for something as mundane as cough syrup or a cup of coffee. Rawley remembered those days. Heavy rain would never be a deterrent to Casey.

"Did the trucker tell you what kind of car?" Rawley asked around the lump forming in his throat.

It was useless getting upset over an unconfirmed suspicion. And his training had kicked in, so while asking the question, he was also running through various scenarios on how the car ended up in the creek; the types of injuries the occupants might have suffered; the damage to the vehicle and/or the bridge.

The amount of rain that had fallen already would have the creek flowing higher so a small car could easily be submerged. A larger vehicle might not have that problem. It all depended on how far into the water the car was sitting. The steep embankment on both sides of the bridge might allow for a vehicle to be only partially submerged. A moment later, Rawley realized Ted had never answered his question. He glanced at his deputy, taking in the man's tense white-knuckle grip, and his anxiety spiked.

"Ted," Rawley barked, using every ounce of authority he could muster through the fear making it hard to breathe. "What kind of vehicle?"

The deputy remained focused on the wet road and worked his jaw, clearly not wanting to answer his boss's question. Ted blew out a loud sigh and then blurted, "It's a gold Mustang."

Rawley's breath seized in his chest and his heart thundered against his ribs. Fear became reality as icy fingers clutched him, threatening to squeeze the life out of him. He folded forward, gripped the dashboard, and forced himself to take slow, measured breaths. He was light-headed. A muzzle flash had him jerking in surprise and remembered pain blossoming in his hip and shoulder. A heavy hand landed on his back and the memory dissipated to be replaced by a horror that was no memory. It had been weeks before he'd learned Alex was gone from his life forever. The family had buried him while Rawley was still in a coma. Rawley had just accepted that loss only to now face the possibility of another.

"Not Casey," he whispered. "It can't be Casey."

"Kane? Boss man, you back with me? Deep breaths."

Ted vigorously rubbed Rawley's back. He followed his deputy's instructions, oxygen sawing through his burning throat. There was only one gold Mustang in Clover City. He knew it was Casey in that creek, but he needed to get his shit together if he was going to help him. No one would benefit from the sheriff losing his shit.

"Almost there," Ted said, glancing quickly at Rawley. "You better now?"

Rawley straightened in the seat and looked at his deputy. "I can't lose him, Ted. I can't lose another man I love."

Ted took his words in stride, nodding slightly while watching the road. Rawley and Ted had always gotten along, might even be friends if Rawley put more effort into it. Rawley respected his top deputy more for his quiet acceptance. He also appreciated that Ted wasn't offering empty promises or false reassurances. There were no words of comfort or claims that Casey would be fine, because in their line of work, they both knew he wouldn't be. Casey would be injured, and those injuries might be life-threatening. Rawley refused to consider the possibility that Casey had been killed. He couldn't.

"I need you to take command because I can't..." Rawley took a deep breath to gain a little more control over the panic, mindlessly rubbing over the scar on his shoulder. "I can barely breathe."

"Yeah, I figured. Why do you think we're in my truck? You're unofficial, boss man."

"But I just told you. How did you know?"

Ted grinned. "You hide it well, but Case? Not so much. He came by the office looking for you the day after you took vacation. When I told him you'd taken a few days off... I don't know. I could just tell." Ted cast a quick look at Rawley that had Rawley lifting his brow in question. "And I might have run into Jake at the post office."

Rawley nodded. He should have expected that.

As they approached the bridge, Ted slowed the Explorer and eased to the side of the road, careful to stay out of the sucking mud that lined the pavement. He parked a good distance from the bridge to leave plenty of room for the first responders to get close. Two patrol cars sat at either end of the bridge, blocking traffic from crossing, not that there would be any. On the other side of the bridge was an eighteen-wheeler stopped right in the middle of the highway, apparently unconcerned about other vehicles. The Mustang wasn't visible due to the steep grade of the creek's edge, and that bothered Rawley. He got out of the truck, ignoring the cold wind and drenching rain, as he made his way to the edge of the embankment. He had to have that visual proof. He had to *know* it was Casey down there hurt, afraid, possibly even dying.

Chapter Twenty-Five

HIS HEART STOPPED at the sight of Casey's car upside down in the water. The damage to the car was fairly extensive, and he knew without doubt that his man was injured badly. When his knees went weak, Ted was beside him instantly, helping him remain on his feet, offering silent support. He stared at the mud as the wind whipped around him, the rain sliding down his neck beneath his collar. His heart thudded in his chest, and his breath came in rapid bursts.

Rawley was alive. He wasn't lying on a dirty sidewalk bleeding, cold numbness spreading through his limbs, while the man he loved died. He wasn't in a coma unaware of what was going on around him or the loss he'd suffered. Not this time. Rawley hadn't been able to help Alex then, but he could help Casey now. Something deep inside him clicked, allowing the panic to ease and his professionalism to take over.

"I'm okay now. Thanks," Rawley told Ted, who nodded.

Rawley took a moment to examine the scene with a critical eye. The car was on its roof at an odd angle, probably due to the unevenly crumpled metal. The front bumper was near the guardrail at the top of the hill where the rail was damaged. There was gold paint transfer embedded in the steel, marking it as the point of impact. Bits of metal and glass of varying sizes were strewn across the muddy embankment. Rawley made a quick scan of the pavement but saw no skid marks, suggesting Casey had never hit the brakes. Damn, he hated single-car crashes. The only ones who really knew what happened were the ones involved, and they either wouldn't or couldn't tell authorities what caused the accident.

Firefighters had already made their way down the hill to the car and were working on prying open the smashed driver's door. The EMTs were unloading the stretcher from the ambulance and assembling the equipment they would need once the firemen extricated Case from the car. All of them worked with calm, focused efficiency. Rawley knew every one of the rescue workers, finding that extremely reassuring, especially since it was Casey they were working to save. He was surrounded by people he knew well, emergency personnel he trusted, a stark contrast to his time in the Denver PD, where those showing up for a call might be complete strangers to him.

Eric, David, and Matt were the firemen; their four-man team was completed by Cameron, who was a firefighter/paramedic. The EMTs who'd responded to the scene were Joe and Leland. Ted had moved halfway down the embankment to keep a watchful eye on the proceedings. Rawley joined him and they both looked on in silence, though with every passing second, Rawley's anxiety rose. The rain was letting up, but the creek level was still higher than normal, moving at a rapid pace. Rawley was incredibly thankful the Mustang had landed with the trunk in the water, rather than the hood or the passenger cabin. The cool temperatures were still a danger to Casey, and Rawley had no idea how long he'd been in this state before the trucker came along.

What-ifs began running through his brain at breakneck speed. What if the car had landed fully submerged in the water? What if that trucker had never come along? Or hadn't been looking in that direction when he crossed the bridge? What if Casey had never been found? Shit, what if it was already too late? Panic once again threatened to overpower him, but he refused to give in. He forced his thoughts in another direction, remembering the way Casey had smiled up at him from the bed that morning. The man had completely changed his life so he could stay in Clover City with Rawley. That's what he chose to think about, what he chose to remember, because he had to believe that Casey was going to be okay. He might be hurt now with a long, difficult road of recovery ahead of him, but he would survive and they'd be together for the rest of their lives.

"You're having your moments, but you're doing surprisingly well with all this," Ted said from beside him.

"It's a struggle, but I won't be any use to him if I lose it."

"What's your take on the scene?" Ted asked.

David used an axe slipped between the bottom of the door and the chassis while Matt used a crowbar near the door handle to finally pry the driver's side door open. The speed with which the men worked told Rawley that Casey was alive, maybe even speaking to them, or their actions would be very different. Rawley suddenly needed to be down by the car so he could pull Casey into his arms as soon as he was free, but he knew that wasn't in Casey's best interests, that he had to stay out of the way. Damn, it was hard not to move. He kept his gaze glued to the rescue as he answered his deputy's question.

"Knowing my man, it was probably excessive speed for the conditions, but I can't be sure. He could've swerved to avoid hitting a dog or something."

"No indication another vehicle was involved?"

"No."

"Yeah, that's what I was thinking, too."

With the loud grating of metal on metal, the vehicle door was finally pulled open. Matt and David stepped aside to allow Cameron, Joe, and Leland to get closer. A cervical collar was passed to Cameron while Joe and Leland prepared the backboard to secure Casey so he didn't suffer further spinal injury. Rawley moved without thought, arriving at the vehicle just as Cameron cut Casey's seat belt. With help from Eric, who had crawled in through the broken passenger window and was lying inside the car on his stomach, they eased Casey's body from the seat. Between the four of them, they managed to get Casey out of the car onto the backboard without jostling or jarring him too badly. Rawley managed to stand back until the men had secured the backboard to the gurney, but then he couldn't stay away. He needed to be close.

The man on the gurney barely resembled Casey, with the extensive bruising, swelling, and blood that covered almost every inch of his body, but Rawley recognized the clothing Casey had been wearing earlier. Both wrists looked to be broken and his left elbow was displaced. Rawley wasn't able to assess other injuries he might have suffered, due to the blood-encrusted clothing, but he wouldn't have been surprised if several more bones were broken. Casey's left leg was lying at an odd angle, and there was a large gash in his thigh. Rawley couldn't swallow around the lump in his throat, tears joined the rain sliding down his face, and his chest tightened painfully. He reached out a shaking hand and carefully brushed his fingers across the back of Casey's hand as he leaned down to whisper in his ear.

"I'm here, Casey. Keep fighting. Don't give up on me now."

Casey didn't respond. While Rawley desperately wanted to hear his voice, he was thankful Casey was unconscious. The pain from his injuries would have been excruciating, and he hoped Casey wouldn't actually regain consciousness until he was in the hospital, where he could be properly medicated and cared for. Joe and Leland flanked the stretcher, while Rawley helped Matt steady the sides, as they all slowly and carefully made their way back up the slick embankment. On more than one occasion, one of them slipped in the mud, forcing the remaining three to struggle with keeping the gurney from dumping Casey onto the ground. Once they reached the top, they were able to lower the wheels so Rawley and Matt backed off to allow Joe and Leland to load Casey into the ambulance.

Ted and the other deputies moved around the scene, taking pictures or gathering other evidence from the accident site. The firemen cleaned up their equipment, but would stick around until the area had been deemed safe so the car could be removed. Dusty was going to hate it, but he'd eventually be called to tow the wrecked Mustang away. In the back of the ambulance, Leland started an IV while Joe tore open Casey's shirt to attach electrodes that would monitor his heartbeat. Rawley stood out in the drizzle as the men worked, wondering if they had become acquainted with Casey yet. It seemed his outgoing and friendly nature would have had him making friends all around town the past three weeks since his arrival. Maybe it was his imagination, but the EMTs seemed to be handling Casey with more care than they typically showed. Did they know what Casey meant to him?

A strong hand landed on his shoulder, jarring Rawley from his thoughts, and he turned to find Ted beside him, attention on the activity inside the ambulance.

"Are you riding with him, boss?"

"I don't know," Rawley answered. He certainly wanted to.

"How about I make the decision for you? Get in that ambulance and be there when he wakes up. I got this handled." Ted squeezed Rawley's shoulder, nodded once, and then returned to supervise the investigation of the wreck.

Rawley climbed into the ambulance just as Joe hopped out to close the doors. While it was procedure for Rawley to show his face at the hospital to interview accident victims, it was unusual for him to accompany the victim in the ambulance, but neither EMT gave any indication they were surprised by his actions. His suspicion that these men knew about his relationship with Casey changed to certainty when Leland offered a sympathetic smile.

"We're taking good care of your man, Sheriff."

"I know you are, Lee. Thank you."

Once the back doors were secured, Joe climbed behind the wheel. Rawley slipped his fingers into Casey's palm, needing a physical connection, no matter how small. He just didn't want to cause more hurt by moving already broken bones. The scent of blood and urine filled the small space, and Rawley suspected the tightening of the lap belt might have caused Casey's bladder to release. He didn't want to consider the internal injuries he might have suffered as the result of the impact. Leland leaned back to check the monitor, which allowed Rawley to lean in closer, gently touching dark hair matted with blood.

"Hang in there, beautiful. We're almost there."

"Heart rate is a little slow, but strong, and his blood pressure is a bit low. All things considered, he's doing okay," Leland told him. "He's a fighter. I have faith he'll pull through just fine."

Rawley truly hoped Leland's assessment was accurate because just the thought of losing Casey made his heart seize in his chest. He'd sunk so far into PTSD-riddled depression after Alex's death, he couldn't begin to imagine how he'd suffer if Casey died. They pulled into the ambulance bay of the hospital moments later, and Rawley relinquished the hold he had on Casey's hand as he was rolled into a storm of emergency-room chaos that would hopefully result in a life long-lived.

Chapter Twenty-Six

AFTER LELAND AND Joe handed off Casey to the ER staff, Rawley stood in the reception area, feeling lost and afraid. As the reality of what happened rushed in on him again, Rawley's legs turned to pudding and he stumbled into a nearby chair. Putting his head in his hands, he quietly broke down. He had no idea how much time had passed before a gentle hand had him lifting his head. Sylvia stood beside him with tears in her eyes. Rawley leaped to his feet and hugged the small woman, each taking comfort in the fact they weren't alone in their distress. Part of Ted's duties as lead was to notify Casey's next of kin, so Rawley should have expected to see Sylvia, but he'd been too lost in his own head. Several minutes later, they broke apart and wiped away their tears.

"How is he?" Sylvia asked.

"He was doing okay in the ambulance, but since we got here...I don't know. I'm not family and I'm not working, so even if I asked, Nancy wouldn't tell me."

Rawley glanced at the woman working the ER reception desk. She was a sweet woman, but she took her job very seriously, especially when it came to patient confidentiality. He'd gone head-to-head with her before and lost. He would get soft words of sympathy, but no information.

"Well, I am family, so I'll go ask." Sylvia patted his arm and walked to the desk.

A murmured conversation and phone call later, Sylvia returned to her seat beside Rawley, taking his hand into hers.

"He's in surgery for an open fracture and knee dislocation. Both wrists were broken and his elbow was dislocated, too, but they were able to just cast those. He has a lot of cuts and bruises, especially on his face, but he doesn't show signs of severe brain injury so that's a good thing."

"It's a damn miracle is what that is," Rawley said. "You should have seen the car, Sylvia. He's lucky to be alive."

Jake flew into the ER waiting room, heading straight for the reception desk as Ryan, who was trailing close behind, noticed them across the room. He grabbed Jake's arm, causing his forward motion to abruptly stop in a comedic one-legged about-face. Ryan caught his boyfriend in his arms before leading him to where Rawley and Sylvia sat. No words were spoken as Sylvia hugged the men. Rawley and Ryan shook hands as Jake and Sylvia dissolved into tears, holding each other.

A few minutes later, Trent, Jordan, and a few other townsfolk Rawley had no idea had befriended Casey showed up at the ER. Everyone took a moment with Sylvia, asking about Casey's condition. Some of them offered Rawley their sympathies, clearly aware of their relationship, before asking him more probing questions about the accident; he was the sheriff, after all. At some point, everyone decided to move into the surgical waiting room, coffee cups and snacks in hand, prepared for a long wait. Rawley sat with Sylvia's hand in his, dazed by the friendship and support Casey was receiving.

What felt like days later, the surgeon announced Casey had been moved to his own room after a successful lower-leg surgery. Only family was allowed to visit at this time, but Rawley's badge earned him entry. When he walked into Casey's room, he was once again thrown by how unrecognizable his boyfriend was. Stitches closed a long cut across his left cheek. His left eye was blackened and swollen shut. Tiny cuts on his neck and upper arms caused by flying glass could be seen where the hospital gown didn't cover skin. His left arm was casted from hand to shoulder to keep both his wrist and elbow immobilized, while the other cast stopped mid-forearm. His left leg was wrapped in bulky postsurgical bandages from thigh to foot, and a thick sock covered his toes. Wires and tubes were attached to several machines that beeped rhythmically, offering proof positive his man was still alive.

Chapter Twenty-Seven

CASEY WAS HOT, his legs and arms heavy. He thought he was paralyzed, but that theory was dismissed when his fingers and toes moved on command, shooting searing pain through his limbs. A gentle voice spoke to him, but he couldn't make out what was being said through the blood rushing in his ears. Seconds later, he was gagging as something was pulled from his throat, that voice calming him the entire time, until the odd obstruction was gone, and he could breathe again. His neck was caressed by large fingers, lessening his discomfort before the same digits slid down to his chest where they rubbed in soothing circles. The pain in his body eased and the noise in his ears subsided so that when the voice spoke again, he recognized it immediately. Rawley was with him.

"You're okay, beautiful."

Casey opened his eyes slowly, blinking rapidly against the light shining directly into his eyes. Correction, eye. He could only see out of his right eye because something was blocking the left. He went to move the offending object to find he could lift his arm, but not bend any of his joints. Panic set in, causing numerous machines to beep incessantly.

"Shh. It's okay, you're okay. Just relax."

He calmed down in increments in response to Rawley's soothing presence. He didn't understand what was going on, or where he was, or why the movement of his limbs was so heavily restricted. There was an uncomfortable pinch in his arm that Casey attempted to move away from only to be stopped by a strong, gentle grip.

"She's just drawing blood. It'll be over in a minute."

"Mr. Holden, can you tell me your name?" asked a woman he couldn't see well due to the blindingly bright lights. Casey couldn't quite comprehend the question.

"You know my name," Casey croaked out. His throat was raw and talking hurt like hell, so he decided not to do much of it.

The woman chuckled. "I do, but do you? I need you to tell me."

"Casey. Why did you bring me here?" he whispered because that hurt a lot less.

"You brought yourself here, honey," the woman said, as she checked his monitors and IV bag. Once his eyes adjusted to the light, he noted the woman was blonde with nice brown eyes and a kind face. "What's the last thing you remember?"

Casey was confused about why this woman was questioning him on stupid things, and why Rawley was allowing such a strange interrogation. "Can we go home? I don't want to be here."

"Not for a while." Rawley's scent filled his nostrils, and he felt warm lips press against his neck below his ear, just the way he liked it. "What's the last thing you remember?" Rawley whispered.

Warmth spread through Casey as he remembered their night together. "You, making love to me."

Rawley laughed softly in his ear as the woman leaning over him blushed. "Do you remember the car accident?" she asked, averting her gaze to something above his head.

"Accident," Casey repeated, turning his head in an attempt to capture more of Rawley's heat, scent, and touch. He would never get enough of Rawley's presence.

"You had a car accident yesterday. Where were you going, beautiful? Do you remember?"

Nothing made sense to him. Rawley and the woman were talking in riddles, but it didn't matter. All that mattered was that Rawley was close, nuzzling his neck, rubbing his chest, and loving him.

"We'll try this again later. He's more coherent every time he wakes up," the woman said to Rawley. "A little thump, Mr. Holden."

Almost instantly Casey felt like he'd been slugged in the hand, the sensation quickly followed by intense fatigue. He fought to stay awake, to enjoy Rawley's lips on him, but no matter how hard he tried, he wasn't able to stay awake.

"It's okay, Casey, go to sleep. I'll be here when you wake up, just like always."

"Okay."

"I love you, beautiful," Rawley whispered in his ear and then kissed his cheek.

"Me, too," Casey mumbled as he fell asleep, Rawley's touch still fresh on his skin and his scent filling his lungs.

IT WAS NEARLY a week before Casey was released from the hospital into Aunt Sylvia's care. She rolled him out to the parking lot, where she immediately turned him over to Rawley, as gorgeous as ever in his sheriff's uniform, causing Casey to smile broadly at him. It pulled the steristrips covering his cheek laceration, but he didn't care. They explained it would be better for him to stay at Rawley's house, where Rawley could assist in bathing and bathroom duties; Aunt Sylvia would come over during the hours Rawley had to work. Casey didn't care why they'd done it, as long as he was with Rawley.

Rawley bent down to brush a soft kiss across his lips, being as gentle and careful as ever. It seemed his boyfriend was terrified of inadvertently hurting him. After some hopping, bumping, jostling, and cursing, mostly on Rawley's part, the three of them managed to get Casey into Rawley's truck and his wheelchair into the bed.

"You know, it would have been easier getting you into a car. Too bad you wrecked yours," Rawley said as he waved at Aunt Sylvia and climbed into the driver's seat.

The truck rumbled to life, and Rawley drove away from the hospital. Casey liked his nurse, Rhonda, and the nurse's aide, John, who came to help him shower and dress every day, but he wasn't sad to be leaving. He was tired of being stuck in one small room. At least at Rawley's house, he could roll his wheelchair outside to enjoy the fresh air, or look at the stars when he couldn't sleep. He missed the stars.

"Do you remember anything about the accident yet?"

It was the same question Rawley and Ted had been asking since he started opening his eyes and talking. He always had the same answer.

"Not really. I know it was raining. I remember being mad because my phone was ringing." Casey tipped his head to the side as the partial memory of a guardrail directly in front of his car popped into his mind. "I think I reached down to answer it and lost control...maybe?" Casey watched out the side window as the street that would take them to Rawley's house passed by. "We're not going home?"

"In a few minutes. I have to stop by the office for a minute. So, you *think* you answered your phone...while you were driving too fast in heavy rain."

Rawley's tone was normal, conversational, but his knuckles were white on the steering wheel. He drove to the police station and pulled into the lot, stopping at an angle so that Casey's side of the truck was facing the front door. Ted came out holding a citation pad, and Rawley rolled down the passenger window. Ted rested his elbows on the door, looking Casey up and down.

"Feeling all right? Doing better?"

"Yes, thank you."

"Don't thank him yet," Rawley told Casey before addressing Ted. "He was driving too fast for the conditions while on...his...cell...phone."

Rawley enunciated the last few words while staring directly at Casey, and Casey knew, without a doubt, the man was pissed. Casey held his boyfriend's gaze until Ted handed him a piece of paper. He took it with his fingers, holding it awkwardly because of the cast, and looked it over.

"You're giving me a ticket?"

"That's not all you're getting, kid, but we'll discuss the rest when you're healed," Ted told him.

"But...for what?"

"Is he serious?" Ted asked Rawley, and Casey glanced at him in shock.

Rawley turned away to stare out the front windshield, leaving it to Ted to explain. Rawley was the sheriff, but apparently, that wasn't going to work in Casey's favor.

"You were driving recklessly, putting other motorists in danger. You totaled your car, littered the creek and hillside with oil and brake fluid, damaged public property, aka the bridge, and you nearly killed yourself. And let's not forget the most important thing—you scared the ever-loving shit out of your boyfriend. The ticket's just the beginning. We'll discuss the real punishment in a few weeks."

Ted smacked the door with an open palm and walked away. Casey let the ticket drop onto the seat next to him, staring at his casted arms and his braced knee, but not really seeing them. He was frustrated that he couldn't remember the accident, but Rawley had shown him pictures of his car, taken at the junkyard. Even without the photos, just the list of injuries the doctor had recited was enough to know it had been bad. Casey jumped in his seat when Rawley threw the truck into park and slammed his hands against the steering wheel. Casey opened his mouth to speak, not really sure what he was going to say, when Rawley climbed out of the cab, leaving the truck idling. He followed the man with his gaze as Rawley stomped around the hood to yank open Casey's door.

Suddenly, he was surrounded by strong arms holding him against a heaving chest. It was an odd position to be held in, but Casey did his best to hug Rawley back.

"Don't you *ever* do that again."

"I didn't mean to," Casey mumbled into Rawley's shirt.

Rawley pulled back, cupped Casey's face, and stared at him with glistening brown eyes. "I've already lost Alex, and I almost lost you. Never again, Casey, promise me you'll never do something stupid like that again. Promise me."

It was a promise beyond Casey's ability to keep. Never getting into another car accident wasn't something he could guarantee, but he could assure Rawley he'd drive more safely. Rawley needed to hear the words, and there was nothing Casey wouldn't do for the man.

"I promise."

Rawley deflated and rested their heads together.

"I love you," Casey said.

Rawley ran his fingers through Casey's hair and kissed his temple. "I love you, too. Now, let's get you home."

About the Author

Kay lives in Colorado with her husband and their animal children. Family is important to her, so there are weekly visits to her parents and frequent text messages with her brothers. She has a severe addiction to coffee and Mexican food.

Kay loves to read and write and can easily become consumed by it for hours, much to the dismay of the husband and dogs. On occasion she can even be convinced to venture out into world of the living.

Email: kaydohertyauthor@gmail.com

Twitter: @kdohertyauthor

Pinterest: @KDohertyAuthor

Other books by this author

Blind Date

Also Available from NineStar Press

Connect with NineStar Press

www.ninestarpress.com

www.facebook.com/ninestarpress

www.facebook.com/groups/NineStarNiche

www.twitter.com/ninestarpress

www.tumblr.com/blog/ninestarpress

www.ingramcontent.com/pod-product-compliance
Lightning Source LLC
Chambersburg PA
CBHW051703180726
48283CB00004B/1195